BRIDE FOR THE TRIBAL CHIEF

Mail Order Brides of Christmas Mountain, Book 3

JO GRAFFORD, WRITING AS JOVIE GRACE

ISBN: 978-1-944794-95-8

GET A FREE BOOK!

Join my mailing list to be the first to know about new releases, free books, special discount prices, Bonus Content, and giveaways.

https://BookHip.com/GNVABPD

ACKNOWLEDGMENTS

Thank you so much to my editor and friend, Cathleen Weaver, for helping me polish this story and make it the best it could be. I'm also grateful to my amazing beta readers, Mahasani and Debbie Turner. Plus, I want to give a shout-out to my Cuppa Jo Readers on Facebook for reading and loving my books!

CHAPTER 1: THE BRIDE PRICE
PECOS

November, 1893 — La Casa foothills, Texas

"How much for a bride?" Chief Pecos had never been one to mince words, and he wasn't about to start today in the middle of some pompous mail-order bride agency. A few days earlier, he'd been shocked to discover such a business existed. *The ways of white men I will never understand.*

He stood in front of the matchmaker's desk, arms crossed, giving the man a hard, measuring look.

Clink Redwood stared defiantly back, his angular jaw going slack with surprise. "I wasn't aware we had an appointment, Mr. Ah..." He slowly rose from his chair, not bothering to wave away the smoke billowing between them. He gave his cigar a few more puffs as he waited for an answer. The resulting smoke rings were nearly as white as his hair.

"Chief Pecos." Pecos didn't so much as blink. No doubt Mr. Redwood hoped to make him cough or step back, which Pecos found both amusing and annoying. He was a Comanche, well accustomed to enduring hours of quiet contemplation in a sweat lodge. It would take more than a little smoke to intimidate him.

Clink's upper lip curled, and the movement created a new set of lines in the papery skin of his face. "An interesting first name. Chief, you say?"

It wasn't immediately clear if the man was trying to be insulting, or if he was simply dull-witted.

"I am a chief," Pecos explained tersely. "Pecos is my name."

"Of course it is!" Mr. Redwood let out a dry cackle. "I was merely testing out a theory."

Oh? Pecos silently waited for him to continue, wondering when they were going to get around to discussing how much it cost to purchase one of the man's ridiculous mail-order bride contracts.

Mr. Redwood straightened to his full, impressive height, bringing them eye-to-eye. "I've been told it's impossible to make a Comanche laugh, so I reckon it's a fact. You didn't so much as smile at my jest."

This time Pecos didn't have to wonder. The matchmaker's mocking tone and expression indicated that the insult was deliberate. "How much for a bride?" he repeated coolly. In the past, he'd pretended to struggle with the English language, mainly to keep the townsfolk at a distance. He wasn't interested in making a bunch of friends. Today, however, he decided to use every ounce of the school-house education his white mother had insisted he receive. He refused to give any more fuel to Clink Redwood's baseless opinions about the "barbarity" of his "savage neighbors to the south." Lord, help him, but he was deathly tired of hearing those phrases!

The man's silvery gaze turned calculating. "Well, now." He hitched his hip on the edge of his desk and continued to smoke as he observed Pecos. He was so thin and gaunt that the fabric of his black suit seemed to bag around him. "First of all, civilized folk do not sit around discussing the price for a woman, as if she's nothing more than a sack of cornmeal."

Oh, I'm the uncivilized fellow here? Chief Pecos felt a vein in his neck twitch at the knowledge he was speaking with a man who made a living out of putting prices on women's heads. As before, however, he kept his silence, allowing the match-maker to dig himself as deep as he wished in his display of poor manners.

Their brief staring contest ended in Mr. Redwood sighing loudly and returning to his seat. He shuffled papers on his desk for several moments while munching and puffing on his cigar. When he finally spoke again, his words were somewhat muffled around the cigar that remained clamped between his teeth. "Well, it's not as if we have a long line of women clamoring to marry you mountain folk." This time he sighed right into his cigar, sending an alarming amount of smoke into the air. "Even so, I'll do what I can for you, if you tell me what sort of wife you're looking for."

Very well. I can make this easy on both of us. "I wish to marry Meg Chastain." *She's exactly what I'm looking for in a wife.* Pecos' heart beat a little harder at the memory of holding her sweet, soft frame in his arms three days earlier.

She'd fallen from the cane chair she'd precariously balanced herself on while trying to reach a high shelf inside the inn's kitchen. Her ankle was broken. He was the fellow who'd found her on the floor and applied the splints and bandage to properly set it.

Mr. Redwood's mouth fell open. "I'm afraid that's not going to be possible. Her hand is already spoken for." He energetically began to comb through the haphazard stacks of paper on his desk, inadvertently knocking one of them over. It went sailing over the side of his desk. Part of the stack fell together with a muted thud, while other papers floated individually through the air like papery birds coming in for a landing on a field of flowers.

Pecos' heart sank. "Indeed?" His voice was cold and clipped, challenging the matchmaker to explain. "When I last saw her this morning, she appeared unwed."

"Yes, yes, of course!" Mr. Redwood sounded harried as he continued to shuffle papers. "Just the other day, however — yesterday, in fact...no, maybe it was two days ago...or three..." His muttering dwindled.

Pecos made no move to fill the awkward silence, hoping the man was vastly uncomfortable with the string of false-hoods he was clearly spinning.

"Aw, hang it, Pecos!" The matchmaker tossed down a handful of papers. "Business ain't been that good lately. These mountain men like the sound of getting married and all, but they sure are slow about coming up with their payments." He gave another long, gusty sigh and seemed to be having trouble meeting Pecos' gaze. "So I had to develop a new system that would allow them to pay installments. There's just one catch. After they've paid fifty percent of what they owe, they get some guarantees."

"Such as," Pecos prodded when he fell silent again.

"Short version of the situation is that Meg's hand is spoken for. So unless you wish to buy out the contracts of a good four to five other fellows, you'll have to get in line for the next bride."

The matchmaker's convoluted explanation as to why Meg Chastain wasn't available to marry, was beginning to sound like a bit of a racket. "How much for Meg?" Pecos demanded, wondering why the man wouldn't just state an amount and be done with it. Pecos had been saving for years from the sale of his Mustangs. He had a generous cash savings stashed in a safe place up the mountain.

Clink Redwood's expression turned sly. "Well, now, I'd

have to do a powerful amount of figuring to come up with that number, and I don't think it's one you'll like."

"How much?" Pecos repeated, suddenly longing to return to the training ring. He decided on the spot that he'd much rather be dealing with a piece of wild, cantankerous horse flesh than the mule-headed matchmaker sitting in front of him — a man his instincts were shouting couldn't and shouldn't be trusted.

"Like I said," the fellow muttered, reaching for his pen. "It'll require me to do some figuring." He dipped his pen in a squatty glass bottle with dried ink rivulets running down the side of it. For the next several minutes, he scratched numbers painstakingly up and down the sheet of paper resting in front of him.

"Alright, then," he finally announced in a satisfied voice. "That should do it." He lifted the paper and waved it in the air to dry the ink. "I can have you married to Meg Chastain by the end of the day," he announced in a tone as smooth as freshly churned butter, "for the sum of five hundred, fifty-two dollars, and seven cents."

Pecos blinked in astonishment, assuming the man was jesting. From what he'd overheard down at Mav's General Store, the cost of a mail-order bride was a $50 down payment to get the process started, followed by another $50 on the day of the wedding.

Mr. Redwood wasn't jesting. He lifted his bony chin and stared back defiantly.

"According to the other fellows in town, that's more than five times what you normally charge." It was akin to highway robbery. Though Pecos had the funds available, he wasn't about to fork over such a ridiculous sum. It was no wonder Mr. Redwood's agency wasn't turning much of a profit lately. He was a sorry excuse for a businessman.

"Like I said, it's a special situation. There's Skip Elder

ahead of you on my waiting list of grooms. Plus Jeremy Mitchel, Matt Griffin, and Thatcher Mills." The matchmaker drummed his fingers on his desk, clearly impatient for the conversation to end.

That was when the truth hit Pecos right between the eyes. For a man so desperate for business, Clink Redwood sure wasn't in a hurry to seal a transaction with him. Pecos resisted the urge to glance down at his fringed buckskin trousers, knowing with sudden certainty that Mr. Redwood's biggest objection was *him*. Since there was no hiding his bronze-skinned heritage, he tipped his hat, deciding on the spot what his next course of action would be. "I'll be back, sir."

It was Mr. Redwood's turn to look surprised. "With the money?" he asked. A hungry shade of hopefulness crept into his beady eyes.

All Pecos did was spin on the heels of his moccasins and exit the small adobe building. *Yes, I'll be returning with the money but not the sum you were hoping for, you fraud!* If he was going to pay more than five times the going rate to acquire Meg as his mail-order bride, he was going to ensure his hard-earned money ended up in the hands of more deserving men than Clink Redwood. A plan was forming in his mind — one that entailed paying off the competition directly in exchange for terminating their contracts. It might not hurt to first run the idea past a friend, though. Fortunately, he knew just the man who would enjoy having his ears bent over such a juicy topic of conversation — good ol' Mav.

Mav Peterson was a lot of things to a lot of people: the proud owner of the General Store, the town's biggest gossip, and a man nearly everyone trusted. Yes, indeed, he was the perfect fellow to consult for a problem like this.

Pecos leaped astride his Mustang, a red and brown steed with bright white speckles, and rode bareback down the winding road to the General Store. A hot, dry breeze was kicking up clouds of dust and sending an occasional tumbleweed rolling down the mountainside.

A sizable cluster of work wagons was parked in front of the store when he arrived, and a half-dozen horses were tethered to the hitching post. Unlike the shiesty matchmaker down the street, Mav Peterson's store was crowded with so many customers that there were actually folks waiting to go inside. And every time a customer crossed the threshold to head back outside, their arms were loaded down with all the bundles and packages they'd purchased — dry goods, tools, bolts of fabric, and more.

Pecos couldn't fail to recognize one wagon in particular — a cheerful green-painted rig with decorative iron wheels. It belonged to the Remingtons, the owners of the newly restored Christmas Mountain Inn. More than likely, Edward had driven his wife, Lacey, into town to shop. She was the first mail-order bride who'd arrived on Christmas Mountain. Iris, the wife of Deputy Jesse Hawling, had been the second.

Now there was Meg, a mail-order bride still waiting to be matched, and Pecos had every intention of being the groom she was matched with.

As he rode closer to the green wagon, he realized that the female sitting alone on the driver's seat was not Lacey, after all, but Meg Chastain — the very woman he was trying to secure as his future bride. She was wearing a pale green dress he'd never seen her in before, one punctuated with a lace collar and ruffles at both the wrists and hem. Not that he didn't like her in it — she was close to taking his breath clean out of his chest — but he couldn't help noting it was a much frillier ensemble than the hired help at Christmas Mountain Inn normally wore.

Fear leaped into his throat at the thought that he might already be too late. Perhaps Clink Redwood had pulled a fast one and had somehow managed to marry her off to another man already, a man who could afford to buy her gifts and dress her in style.

She glanced up as he brought his horse to a standstill beside the wagon. "Hello, Pecos." There was an underlying note of shyness in her voice, and her tree bark-colored eyes were swimming with curiosity.

Two Dark Moons. It was what he secretly called her, since her lovely eyes constantly haunted his thoughts and dreams. To his enormous relief, there was no wedding band encircling her finger. She wore no jewelry at all.

Alas, no flowery words flooded across his tongue in the way of a return greeting. He'd not been born with a silver tongue, so he decided to stick to his usual methods and get straight to the point. "I met with Clink Redwood this morning. He says there are four grooms in line ahead of me, all with a claim on your hand." He wished he had better news to give her, but experience had taught him that the truth was usually best.

Her rose petal lips parted in shock. "Four!" she gasped, turning a few degrees paler. Her left leg was stretched out from the bench on some sort of makeshift ledge, her ankle swathed in a thick white bandage. "How in tarnation can that old reprobate make such a heinous claim? Why, I'm of a good mind to—" She broke off whatever she was about to say, leaning forward to dig her fingers in her knee as if it pained her.

He swiftly leaped down from his horse, confident the beast was too well trained to run away. "Are you alright?" He advanced on Meg, eyeing her injured ankle in concern.

"No, Pecos! I am not!" she snapped. "A few months ago I had my reasons for signing that blasted mail-order bride contract. Good reasons! Or so I thought. In hindsight, I wish I'd have just kept running." She winced as she glanced down at her swollen ankle. "That's exactly what I would be doing right now if I could." Her voice shook on the last word, making her clamp her lips in defiance.

Running? His gaze narrowed on hers as he absorbed the extent of her agitation. Though he was thrilled by the discovery she had no interest in marrying any of Mr. Redwood's prospective grooms, her words indicated she was in some sort of trouble. He waited for her to explain, but she fell silent.

Grimacing, he confessed, "I am glad you did not keep running from whatever trouble you're in." *And that you're currently in no position to do so.*

"Why does it matter to you?" she cried. The hand she waved at him trembled. "If there truly are four would-be grooms ahead of you on Clink Redwood's blasted list, there's not a chance in the world we'll be allowed to wed."

Allowed? Pecos didn't care one bit for the defeat he heard in her voice. He lifted his chin. "I'm not asking his permission. Only yours, Two Dark Moons."

Her pouty lips opened, closed, and opened again. "Two Dark Moons?" she murmured in wonder. "Why did you call me that?"

The mountain breeze whistled between them, whipping at the soft tendrils of dark hair dangling against her cheeks. His fingers itched to reach up and smooth them away from her face.

"Your eyes," he explained, feeling awkward. "They are dark, yet full of light."

"It sounds like poetry." She suddenly sounded a bit winded. "And it's so much lovelier than plain old Meg."

He couldn't have agreed more. Whoever had christened her with such a simple name had done her a great disservice. The sounds of men's voices and the whinny of horses around them faded as he focused his attention solidly on the woman in front of him.

"But I don't see how it matters who I wish to marry. So long as I'm bound by that horrible contract…" Her voice dwindled helplessly, and her dark, expressive eyes were full of unspoken apologies.

"It matters to me." If he was going to spend more than five hundred dollars and risk bringing the wrath of the law down on his head, he needed to be sure that Meg did, in fact, wish to marry him as much as he wished to marry her.

"What exactly are you asking?" she whispered.

He met her bashful gaze and held it. "I am asking you to marry me."

"I-I can't." She shook her head. "You heard the man. I am sorry."

Because you think you're trapped in a bridal contract, yes. "But if you could?"

"Yes. Of course I would, Pecos." She bit her lower lip, looking shy again. And slightly mortified by her outburst…

It was probably as close as he'd ever come to smiling. "Then I shall eliminate the competition."

She caught her breath, raising her blushing face to his. Cautious hope warred with the discouragement in her gaze. "That sounds ominous."

"More like expensive." He took a step closer to gently rest his hand on top of the one she had gripping the wagon seat. "Mr. Redwood said I could buy out the other four contracts."

Her lips twisted in indignation. "So that's what he really wants!" she declared bitterly. "Money. More than he's due." She shook her head in disgust. "What a racket he has going on!"

"Agreed." Pecos gently squeezed her hand before letting it go. "However, that isn't the issue. You are worth the price to me. Any price."

Her dark, silky brows flew upward. "You think I'm worth four contracts?"

"Five, actually." Clink Redwood hadn't hesitated to heap the full price of another whole contract into the mix, claiming Pecos needed to pay for his own contract in addition to buying out the other four.

"That's highway robbery!" She looked aghast. "Though I am flattered beyond belief that you find me worthy of such a high price, you simply can't pay it and let the cad get away with such nonsense."

"I wasn't planning on it," he assured softly. "I'm heading inside to discuss it with Mav, but I'm of the mind to pay off the other fellows directly. Sure, it'll still cost me the same, but it won't line Mr. Redwood's pockets in the process."

Meg let out a breathy trill of laughter that he found to be a thousand shades of enchanting. "You would do that for me?"

"In a heartbeat." He didn't need time to think about his answer. He was that certain about his feelings for her.

"But we barely know each other." She waved her hands the way she always did when she spoke. He wondered if she even realized she was doing it. "You've only been delivering milk to the inn for how long?" She looked deliciously off balance and frazzled as she shot him an inquiring peek from beneath her long lashes.

"Three months, four days, and two hours," he supplied, still holding her gaze. The fact that a Comanche chief had been performing the menial task of delivering milk to the inn, was the source of no small amount of jests among the members of his tribe. However, he'd refused to turn the chore over to someone else. It was the only way he'd been able to guarantee seeing her each day.

She blushed at his words. "You were counting?"

"Yes."

Her blush deepened. "We never exchanged three words until the day I fell and broke my ankle." She spoke in a low, uncertain voice.

"Are a bunch of words truly necessary?" he asked her tenderly.

"For me?" She blinked up at him, finally meeting his gaze more fully. "Yes. I would like to know the man I am going to marry. I want to know what you like and dislike, Pecos. I want to know the things that inspire you and make you happy. I want to know what you're thinking, and..." She caught her lower lip between her teeth again.

"I like you. You make me happy. I am thinking about you. What other questions do you have of me, Two Dark Moons?"

"So many." She gave another one of her delighted trills of laughter. "A few dozen, at least."

"If you marry me, we will have the rest of our lives together for me to answer them," he returned evenly, "but not unless I beat the rest of my competition to the altar, and that is going to require Mav's help, I think."

"Or mine." Her voice dropped to a soft, silky note.

He studied her curiously, waiting for her to elaborate.

"I may not own much more than the clothes on my back, Pecos, but I am not entirely without resources."

He had no idea what she was talking about.

"In fact, I could probably get every one of those other would-be grooms to withdraw their contracts without you having to spend a penny on them."

Dare I ask? "How?"

Another gust of wind swirled between them, riffling the hem of her skirt. With a small expulsion of irritation, Meg clapped both hands down on the fabric to hold it in place. Despite her efforts, the breeze lifted the ruffled hem from her ankles, making it flutter down against her hands.

"I'm not certain you would understand." She sounded

rueful. "It's about propriety and hoity-toity-ness, things that might not even matter to many folks this far west."

He folded his arms. "Try me."

"Very well." Still blushing, she lifted her head from her blowing skirts to meet his gaze once again. "I could spread the word that you and I have an understanding."

"About what?" He felt like she was speaking in riddles.

Her blush deepened. "About getting married, you silly man!"

"Ah." An understanding. Well, that was one way of looking at his marriage proposal.

"I will spread the word that you asked me to marry you, that I said yes, and that we are vastly in love with each other."

No, you are not. Not yet, anyway. "Why would you lie?" Sure, he had plans to make the lovely creature in front of him fall in love with him someday, but...

Anger tinged her cheekbones a different shade of pink than before. "I would not be spreading falsehoods! I distinctly recall you asking me to marry you, sirrah!"

And I distinctly recall you saying yes, my precious little spitfire. "That I did, but I am not fool enough to assume a simple question was enough to make you fall in love with me." That would come later, Lord willing.

"Fine!" she shot back. "I am not in love with you or any other man."

Ouch! The woman sure didn't sugar coat things. He liked hearing that her heart wasn't already engaged elsewhere, though.

"It hardly matters for what I have in mind. Folks only need to *think* we are in love."

"I am all ears." He'd never in his life been so amused or so intrigued.

"It's going to require a bit of a demonstration, of course, to get folks to believe us."

Oh? Her face was so red by now that he couldn't wait to hear what part he would be playing in her little game.

"Would you step closer, Pecos? I've no wish to fall out of the wagon while I, that is, while w-we…" she stammered into silence.

He immediately stepped to her side, gazing at her anxiously. "Are you well?" She looked close to swooning. Maybe that was why she was sounding so addled all of a sudden. Should he go fetch the town doctor?

She swayed closer. "Pecos," she murmured, sounding short of breath as she reached for his shoulders. "Pray do not mistake me for a woman of loose morals, because I can assure you I've never done anything like this before."

"Like what?" he muttered. There was something about her nearness that was doing strange things to his brain. It was harder to think when she was this close to him. Harder to breathe. Harder to do anything but drown in her beautiful eyes and sweet, flowery scent.

In that moment, there was nothing he wouldn't have done to marry her. No price he wouldn't have paid. No dragon he wouldn't have battled to win her hand. Whatever she was asking of him, it was hers for the taking. *He* was hers for the taking.

"Like this," she cried softly. Her pale, fine-boned features drifted closer, making his heart pound with awareness — the man-to-woman kind of awareness.

Then her rosy lips touched his.

CHAPTER 2: THE BOUNTY
MEG

Meg's heart turned a dozen flips forward, then a dozen flips backward, and a few more sideways as Chief Pecos indulged her, without hesitation, in the first kiss of her adult life.

He canted his head to avoid bumping her with the brim of his brown leather Stetson. His hard mouth settled against hers and unexpectedly gentled as he absorbed her shockingly bold move.

She sensed a suppressed energy in him, one that he was holding brutally in check. That's when she realized he was kissing her back, but just barely.

As quickly as she'd initiated the kiss, he broke it off and pulled back.

"Meg," he muttered regretfully. "We cannot do this."

"We just did," she snapped, feeling close to tears. What was wrong with him? She'd just finishing baring her heart and soul to him and risked shredding every last vestige of her reputation on his behalf. If he denied what was happening between them now, or worse — changed his mind about marrying her — she would be utterly ruined.

"I meant we should not have," he corrected gently. "Not here. Not now."

Well, she supposed that was better than denouncing their kiss altogether. "Why not?" Feeling petulant, she glanced swiftly around them to discover a half-dozen scruffy mountain men staring in their direction. Varying degrees of curiosity and outrage mottled their features.

"It is not safe, Meg. Trust me." His voice was low and cautious, without much inflection.

Returning her gaze to his, she was struck by the storm of emotions broiling in his dark eyes. His normal stoicism was utterly gone. She was heartened to discover he was no more immune to their kiss than she was.

Oh, but her own heart was in trouble! It raced like a runaway horse at how handsome he was in his buckskins. Most men wouldn't have done the look justice, but his fringed trousers and moccasins suited him to perfection. A hand-crafted leather belt, with an interesting geometric design etched into it, was slung around his hips. A holster was attached to it with a silver pistol strapped inside. She resisted the urge to press her palms to her hot cheeks at the breadth of his shoulders and chest. She could almost hear the seams of his buckskin jacket straining from all the muscles bulging and bunching beneath it.

"We're in broad daylight," she protested, drinking in the sleek, black mane of hair flowing past his shoulders, "right in the center of town." How could they possibly be in any danger?

"Precisely." He took another step back, holding up his bronze hands as if surrendering to her.

Then she understood. The danger he was referring to was the one she was putting him in. Another hasty glance around them revealed that two cowboys were fingering the pistols stuffed in their holsters.

"I only meant to lay my claim on you," she sputtered, scanning the hard angles of his features. "To make it known that I am yours and you are mine." *Oh, my lands!* The very idea of belonging to a man like him took her breath away all over again.

"Mission accomplished, ma'am," he assured quietly.

She chuckled at the prim title. "Not quite, but it's a small town," she continued in a breathy voice, "people will gossip."

"That they will." Answering amusement glinted in his coal gaze. "I reckon everyone in town will have heard about our kiss come nightfall. Are you certain that is what you want? I like Mav Peterson and all, but you kissed me in full view of his shop window. There is no way he missed it."

And anyone who knew Mav Peterson knew how much the middle-aged store owner adored gossiping.

"I am." She could feel herself blushing again. "So long as you intend to keep your end of the deal and marry me, that is exactly what I want."

"I am a man of my word, Meg. Everyone who knows me can vouch for that. The Remingtons, Mav Peterson, Deputy Hawling... Well, I reckon you can't ask him these days."

She pounced on the name, anxious to learn more about Chief Pecos' relationship with the deputy who'd been missing from their small town for months now. "How well did you know Jesse Hawling?" she pressed, wishing she'd arrived in town a few months earlier. Maybe then she'd have gotten to meet the notorious deputy who'd supposedly helped his wife escape from being committed to an insane asylum. There were other rumors, too — ones that claimed he'd once served a stint at the asylum, himself.

"Well enough to know he was a good man," Chief Pecos informed her quietly. "The townsfolk suffered a tremendous loss the day he left Christmas Mountain."

"What about the charges of insanity?" She stared. She'd

heard his wife's family had been ready to lock her up and throw away the key.

"I reckon I've been around long enough to know there are two sides to every story, Meg. Sometimes three. Yours, mine, and the truth."

"I like how you think." She was wildly impressed by his matter-of-fact attitude and flawless logic. No doubt about it, she was about to hitch herself to a very wise man. It was no wonder his tribe had chosen him to be their chief.

"Speaking of my side of the story." He caressed her with his eyes. "I truly do need to confer with Mav Peterson." He squinted through the glaring sun at her. "About how to best handle Clink Redwood."

"You should do nothing," she protested. Hadn't she just finished explaining that to him? Men could be so dense sometimes! "Just wait and give the tale of our kiss time to circulate a bit around town."

The door to the General Store abruptly opened and closed. "Meg!" Edward Remington strode in her direction. "We need to talk." A normally even-tempered man, he sounded unaccountably worried.

The tall, dark-headed innkeeper carried himself with an Old World dignity that revealed his aristocratic roots. Though an American citizen, he had British blood running through his veins and a staunch East Coast accent to go with it. His wife, Lacey, was clinging to his arm. She was a petite dewdrop of a woman who looked as if the next mountain breeze might blow her clear into the adjacent county. Though she'd made an attempt to pin her mess of red-gold curls into an up-do, the silky strands were fast sliding from their confinement. Interestingly enough, the lace and green wool ensemble billowing from beneath her cloak was made from the same bolt of fabric as the one Meg was wearing. The woman had generously insisted on having a new gown made for them both.

"What is it?" Meg stiffened her spine, pulling herself up straight on the hard wagon bench. No doubt Edward and Lacey had witnessed her kissing Chief Pecos. A small thrill of fear worked its way through her at the possibility that they might fire her on the spot for exhibiting such impropriety.

Please don't. I need my job at the inn. She needed the room and board that came with it, as well as the meals — at least until she and Pecos were married.

"This!" Lacey lifted and waved the piece of paper she'd been clutching at her side. She spared Chief Pecos a quick, harried flicker. "You might as well follow us back to the inn, Pecos. If what I think I saw through the store window really happened, this concerns you as much as it concerns Meg."

So you did see our kiss. It didn't look as if they planned to fire her over it, though.

Pecos gave a brief nod but didn't answer, to Meg's chagrin. Now was certainly not the time for the man to be silent on the topic of their "understanding."

Swallowing a sigh, she stretched out a hand for the mysterious piece of paper. Lacey relinquished it to her, and she found herself staring down at a WANTED poster. *Please, God, no!* The face of the accused stared back at her in defiance, making her hands shake. How in Heaven's name had her worst nightmare caught up to her in such a small, rural town? Christmas Mountain was well off the beaten track, which was why she'd chosen to hunker down here in the first place. Of all the rotten luck to have a bounty notice drift this far!

"You look as if you've seen a ghost, my dear. Do you know the man in the picture?" Lacey chattered in excitement as her husband lifted her into the wagon. "Everyone in the store was exclaiming about how your resemblance to him is uncanny! I assured Mav it was nothing more than a coincidence, but I wouldn't mind hearing it from your own lips." She took a seat on a bale of hay behind the driver's seat, spreading her full skirts carefully around her. The kindhearted gesture allowed Meg to remain up front with her leg extended on the wooden contraption Edward had commissioned Jonah Hawling to build for her. He'd more or less completed the job on the sly, since the Hawlings and Remingtons were pretending to be at odds with each other in public — a state of affairs Meg did not yet fully understand.

After untethering his horses, Edward eased his tall frame onto the bench beside her. He threw a glance over his shoulder to ensure his wife was settled before lifting the horses' reins. "Giddy-up!" His team edged away from the front of the General Store and clip-clopped their way up Main Street.

Meg felt the air seep from her lungs as she continued staring at the poster in her hands. She could feel Pecos' gaze on her as he rode bareback beside the wagon on his Mustang. *What am I going to tell my employers? And Pecos?* Her innate sense of self-preservation was urging her to spin a falsehood, to simply deny what she was looking at. Lacey had already given her the perfect way out by claiming to a store full of people that Meg's resemblance to the wanted man was mere coincidence.

But it was so much more than that. Meg knew exactly whose face was plastered across the poster. "I do know this person." She was still working up the nerve to raise her gaze from the paper.

"My lands, Meg!" Lacey's voice sounded so close that Meg jumped. She'd not realized her employer's wife was leaning over her shoulder in an attempt to get another look at the face on the poster. "Who is he?"

"It's not a man," Meg supplied in a dull voice. "It's a woman dressed as a man." Back in her bounty hunting days, she'd often cross-dressed as a cowboy. It was the only way to be taken seriously in that line of business. The only person who'd known her true identity had been her business partner, the man who'd ultimately betrayed her.

And so the huntress became the hunted.

A woman who'd taken so much pride in upholding and enforcing the law, Meg had certainly never expected to see her own face staring back at her from a WANTED poster.

I am doomed! A sheen of tears temporarily blinded her as she glanced piteously at the broken ankle that was currently holding her prisoner. *I cannot run this time.* Her mind raced over her dwindling list of options, briefly entertaining and discarding the notion of stealing a horse to make her getaway in a saddle. *But all that would do is add kindling to the lies he's spreading about me.* Not to mention it would turn her into exactly what he was accusing her of being — a lowdown criminal. She was many things and not all of them perfect, but she was innocent of the accusations stamped in cold, straight letters beneath the black-and-white photograph of her:

$2500 for the capture of the man who robbed Midtown Bank in Riverville. Believed to be armed and dangerous. May be a member of Jesse James' Band or the Youngers. Wanted dead or alive. Contact the Sheriff of Dry Gulch County, Texas.

Two thousand five hundred dollars! It was a king's ransom! Meg's insides trembled with horror. Her ex-partner, Jones Storm, must be getting desperate if he was forking out that much cash to sic the bloodhounds of justice on her. The price he'd placed on her head was high enough to bring every bounty hunter and his cousin scurrying out of the woodwork, including all the less-than-honorable scallawags who couldn't care less about upholding the law. They were only in it for the money; she would not escape with any breath left in her. She could rest assured Jones was counting on it.

Dead or alive, my hide! She knew the truth. The man, who was trying to frame her for his own crimes, wanted her six feet under the dirt. That way she'd take the blame for all his double-dealing while he scuttled away in the shadows with the loot from his side hustle.

What changed you, my friend? Meg would have given anything to know. She and Jones had grown up at the same orphanage. Once upon a time they'd been as close as siblings. Folks would've probably assumed they were exactly that if it weren't for one small detail. He was black, and she was white; but they were every bit as close as family, maybe closer. And they'd always had each other's backs. Until they hadn't...

As the tang of betrayal filled Meg's mouth all over again, she swayed in her seat. Lacey's questions faded to a dissonant sing-song from behind her.

"Meg!" The shout from Chief Pecos made her blink. From the corner of her eye, she caught a blur of movement. Then the wagon sank on one side beneath his weight as he leaped from his horse to the bench where she was sitting.

At a sharp command from him, his speckled Mustang continued to trot obediently alongside the wagon.

"I am here," he declared in a low voice, banding Meg with his arms.

She leaned into his strength, allowing her head to dip against his shoulder. "Tear it up," she whispered, fisting the dreadful poster against his chest. "It's nothing but lies. We need to find every one of them and destroy them all." Otherwise, both of their lives were about to become a living hell. Because of their kiss, she'd pulled him into the flames with her.

"I will." His arms tightened around her, underscoring his promise.

"It *is* you on the poster, isn't it?" Lacey demanded incredulously from behind them. "It's really and truly you, my dear?"

"Yes." Meg squeezed her eyelids shut, trying valiantly to hold back the tears. She failed, and they came skidding hotly out from beneath her lids. "But I can explain," she quavered. *Good gracious! If I'd robbed a bank, I certainly wouldn't be living in the middle of some God-forsaken mountain town, scrubbing pots and pans for a living.* However, she knew how pathetic her claims of innocence would sound. Every thief, horse rustler, and fraudster she'd ever run across had proclaimed their innocence — loudly — right up to the point they were clapped behind bars or strung up by a rope.

"There has to be some mistake." Lacey's voice was shrill with indignation. "If anyone asks me, I'll happily set them straight on the matter. I've never encountered a more trustworthy soul than yours."

"Thank you," Meg murmured damply against Pecos' shoulder. She fought to collect her scattered emotions. "I certainly wouldn't have needed to sign a mail-order bride contract if I'd robbed a bank, would I?" She chuckled despite the gravity of the situation. The return of her humor gave her the strength to lift her head once again. "Pray forgive me for being such a watering pot." As Edward turned onto the gravel drive leading up to the inn, she gripped Pecos' steely upper arms to steady herself.

He didn't answer; he merely watched her in quiet contemplation, allowing her to make use of his sturdy self to counteract the jostling. Her gaze inevitably dipped to his mouth as she remembered their kiss. The grim line of his lips made her face heat. He wasn't nearly as hard as he came across; there was tenderness in him, too. She'd felt it for the briefest of moments, and was already longing to revel in it again.

The way Pecos' eyes darkened told her he was remembering, too.

Allowing her lashes to flutter against her cheeks, she wiped the dampness from her face with the back of one hand. "I was merely wallowing in a moment of self pity." But no longer. She straightened her spine and dragged in a breath, ready to share the rest of her story. Lacey and Edward had been nothing but kind to her; they deserved the truth. So did the man she was preparing to marry. That is, if he still wanted to marry her after learning her real reason for coming to town...

"Pecos," she pleaded softly, willing him to be understanding of what she was about to impart.

For an answer he held his hand up between them, beckoning her to take it. After a short hesitation, she reached up to press her palm to his, and he laced his fingers through hers. Though he still didn't say anything, she was comforted by the knowledge that he wasn't utterly repelled about finding her picture on a WANTED poster.

"I will tell you everything," she promised in the same soft voice.

His frown didn't waver, but his fingers tightened over hers.

The narrow, winding path led uphill for a bit, then flattened out across a vast plateau. In the distance rose a white two-story structure. They'd arrived at Christmas Mountain Inn. According to Edward, it had been a dilapidated disaster upon his arrival out west to claim his inheritance. One would never guess from the looks of it now.

The walls wore a fresh coat of white paint, the glass windows were polished to a sparkle, and the wooden shutters were stained a warm shade of honey-oak. It was a homey, restful scene — one that Meg had been in no dashing hurry to leave before today. The deer and caribou grazing through the craggy mountain grasses at daybreak and sunset were truly a breathtaking sight. And oh, what a view the mountains provided! The towering, rocky ridges were smudged with reds and golds in the early morning and blues and purples during the latter part of the day. Since the November nights were quickly fading to December, Meg knew it was only a matter of time before the mountains would be capped in white.

She'd been longing to see the town of Christmas Mountain dressed in snow and could only hope the WANTED poster wouldn't chase her away before she had the chance to.

"Let's convene in the back parlor," Lacey ordered briskly, while her husband lifted her down from the wagon.

Pecos leaped to the ground but made no effort to assist Meg, likewise. Instead, he scooped her into his arms, as if she weighed no more than a kitten, and strode wordlessly with her toward the porch stairs.

"My crutch is in the back of the wagon," she pointed out, breathless at the pleasure of being in his arms again. Mercy, but she'd never been one to sigh and simper over a set of manly arms. Until now. Until Pecos.

"I'll return for it."

She turned her head his way to thank him and found her mouth devastatingly close to his again.

"No need," Edward assured from behind them. "I have it in hand."

Meg couldn't find the voice to answer. It was stuck in her throat at the raw passion she read in Pecos' gaze. Her heart gave a crazy answering flutter from beneath her ribs. She wanted so badly to lean an inch or two closer and touch her mouth to his again, to find out if his lips would go all tender against hers like they had the first time.

His dark gaze boldly plundered hers as he carried her up the porch stairs and down the plank hallway toward the rear of the inn.

Her blush spread from her cheeks to her neck at the admiration and sheer maleness oozing from him.

"So…" Lacey gazed curiously between the two of them as they entered the Remington's private parlor. No guests were allowed back here, only family and close friends. She smoothed her hair from her face as Pecos set Meg gently on the sofa. "It appears you have an understanding, eh?"

Meg smiled tremulously up at Pecos as he straightened. "He asked me to marry him, and I said yes."

"Oh, how wonderful!" Lacey clapped her hands, beaming with pleasure at the news. "Though I must ask, how is this going to work with your mail-order bride contract?" Her smile slipped. "I thought Clink already had you promised to another man."

"He does." Meg rolled her eyes. "As a matter of fact, he has me promised to no less than four hopeful grooms on his ever-growing list."

"Say it isn't so!" The innkeeper's wife recoiled in astonishment. "Clink may not be the brightest apple in the barrel, but even he must know he cannot split you four ways." She sank into a velvet Queen Anne chair across from the sofa, watching with interest as Pecos propped Meg's injured ankle on a pillow.

Meg shrugged. "I've been suspicious for weeks that he's merely using me to drum up more business." Her mouth tightened. "I don't believe he's been trying very hard to marry me off to any one man in particular. To be perfectly honest, I initially feared you might be in on the charade, too." She lowered her gaze sheepishly.

"Me?" Her hostess pressed a hand to her bosom, looking perplexed. "Why, I wouldn't trust Clink Redwood if he was the last man on earth." She made a face. "Do recall I had to deal with the man, as well, when I first came into town." She was the first mail-order bride who'd arrived at Christmas Mountain.

Edward waggled his dark brows at her. "If it's any

comfort, my precious wife, he charged me double his current going rate for you." He shook his head. "It was before he'd published his price list."

"It's no comfort to me," Meg retorted dryly, making both Lacey and Edward chuckle. "Pecos approached him for my hand in marriage this morning, and he's trying to charge more than five times what his contract states."

"Good heavens! What a despicable creature!" Lacey leaned back to pull the chain against the wall to call for tea. It took her a moment to recall that Meg was sitting directly across from her and that no tea service would be forthcoming. She bobbed back to her feet. "I reckon it's up to me to set the water boiling."

Edward muttered something about needing to complete a quick errand and rushed off to his office, leaving Meg and Pecos alone.

He stood against the far wall, arms crossed as he silently regarded her. He'd been patient so far, not demanding answers from her, not demanding anything at all. However, she knew he deserved to know her story.

"I was raised in an orphanage," she blurted, "and eventually became a bounty hunter." Encouraged by the spark of interest in his gaze, she plunged onward. "I was good at what I did, bringing bad hombres to justice and collecting their bounties. My partner was a man by the name of Jones Storm. He was raised at the same orphanage. He was like a brother to me." Her voice turned sad. "Somewhere along the way, he changed, though. He must have gotten tired of collecting minuscule bounties, while watching so many criminals grow rich — bank robbers, highwaymen, and horse thieves." Her voice shook with emotion as she plowed on. "The accusations listed on the poster should be directed at him. Not me. Why he wishes for me to take the fall for what he did is a mystery." In times past, he would've taken a bullet before letting any harm come her way. Her heart still bled, just thinking about it.

The empathy smoldering in Pecos' dark gaze was all the encouragement she needed. The rest of her story came spilling out. "The accusations blew up out of nowhere, and Jones disappeared, leaving me to face them alone. So I did what any orphan without connections would do; I ran." Technically, she'd done more than that. She'd signed a mail-order bride contract and traveled to Christmas Mountain to marry a complete stranger. It was a rash thing to do, but she'd been that desperate to start fresh some place else. And she certainly didn't have enough money to travel on her own dime.

Already she regretted it, though. She wished she could pull up the proverbial tent stakes and simply keep running. "If I hadn't been foolish enough to fall off that cane chair..." Her voice dwindled in misery.

"What? So you could leave us?" Lacey demanded, returning to the parlor with a fancy silver tray in hand. Tiny tea cakes were artfully arranged around a floral teapot.

"Well, yes." Meg turned to her hostess in shame. "Pray forgive me. No doubt it seems ungrateful after all you and Edward have done for me."

"You're afraid, is all," Lacey assured, setting the tray down on the short table in front of Meg. "I know I would be if our roles were reversed."

While she poured a round of tea, Edward rejoined them. "What did I miss?" He accepted the cup his wife offered him and swiveled expectantly in Meg's direction.

"I was a bounty hunter," she sighed. "One of the best, if you can suffer a little bragging. That is, until my partner betrayed me."

CHAPTER 3: HER HIDING PLACE

PECOS

C hief Pecos watched Edward Remington closely as Meg Chastain unfolded the fascinating story about her past. He waffled between fury on her behalf and admiration over her bravery. The woman he wanted to marry was so much more than a beautiful face. Her fine-boned features and delicate hands masked an indomitable strength that rivaled the toughest men he'd ever come across — a strength, most unfortunately, that had not been immune to the ricketiness of one old cane chair.

It was wrong of him, but Pecos was actually grateful to the spindly piece of furniture that had grounded the lovely bounty hunter sitting before them. If it were not for her injury, he had no doubt that she would be long gone from his life by now. Instead, she was at his and Edward Remington's mercy, a responsibility he didn't take lightly.

When she paused her tale to take a sip of her tea, Pecos caught Edward's eye. "Are Clink Redwood's mail-order bride contracts on the right side of the law?" Before Edward had traveled west to lay claim to the inn he'd inherited from his grandfather, he'd studied to become a lawyer. He was well-versed in many legal matters.

Edward's jaw tightened. He was standing next to the fireplace with one elbow propped on the mantle. Behind him was a set of floor-to-ceiling shelves crammed with books. "I was wondering the same thing." He blew on his tea as he returned his attention to Meg. "I don't reckon you have a copy of the one you signed?"

At her shame-faced head shake to the contrary, he gave a short huff of disgust. "I figured as much. Clink doesn't impress me as the kind of fellow who'd want to leave a paper trail of his shenanigans."

His wife set her teacup down on the tray with a clatter. "Are you saying nothing can be done about the man's despicable business practices?" She swiped a hand angrily through the air. "Charging one fellow this and another fellow that?" She pointed at Pecos. "Then sticking our local Comanche chief with a bill that's more than five times the going rate?"

Edward's dark eyebrows shot upward. "I reckon you can pen a contract between folks about most anything, but he's still walking a very fine line between what's legal and what's not. A good lawyer wouldn't have too much difficulty challenging his position on the matter."

"I cannot afford a lawyer," Meg interjected sharply. "Since I did *not*, in fact, rob any banks and do *not* have a large pile of cash stashed anywhere."

"I can think of one attorney in particular who might take on your case, with or without cash," Edward returned smoothly.

Lacey gave a girlish squeal of excitement. She sat forward in the blue velvet chair, gazing adoringly across the room at her husband. "I knew you would think of a way around this, sweetheart. I just knew it!"

He gave her a tender smile while continuing to speak to Meg. "If you hire me to represent you, Meg, I'll file a grievance on your behalf, demand a copy of your mail-order contract from Clink, and see what I can do about terminating your ties to him."

"Hire you with what?" she sputtered. "As much as I appreciate the kindness of your offer, I am not a charity case." She was poor, but her orphanage days were long behind her. She'd been earning her own way for the past five years.

"I said with or without cash," he reminded. "But if you insist on compensating me for my services, you can work it off at the inn." He looked in askance at Pecos, as if to gauge his level of approval. "I know you're about to get married, but I am hoping not to lose you from the inn staff just yet. At least, not before we can hire a proper replacement."

She shot him a grateful look. "It's not that I mind being useful, sir, but I am about to have a whole army of bounty hunters descending on my ears." She uncrumpled the poster she'd been clutching and waved it at him. "Though they are false accusations, I am currently one of the most wanted persons in the west."

He grimaced. "I can't imagine anyone in their right mind would believe such a thing about you."

"It doesn't matter what you or I believe," she pointed out bleakly. She refolded the poster, creasing it into smaller and smaller squares before allowing it to drop into her lap. "That size of a bounty is going to keep a set of crosshairs on my forehead I won't be able to dodge forever. Heaven knows I've tried."

Pecos figured he'd kept his silence long enough. "As a precaution, we should return to town and remove every one of those posters."

"Agreed." Edward pushed away from the mantle. Moving to the center of the room, he stooped to deposit his empty teacup on the tray. "I'll pay the sheriff a visit while we're in town and see what he has to say about things." At Meg's sharp intake of breath, he hastened to assure, "Don't worry. He can be trusted."

"It also might not hurt to make Mav Peterson aware of our dilemma," Pecos pointed out. "When he talks, folks tend to listen." Mav's word could squash a rumor as quickly as it could start one. Plus, Pecos still wouldn't mind getting Mav's insight on Clink Redwood. Though a lot of folks in town seemed to like him, Pecos' instincts told him there was something fishy going on with the fellow.

"Agreed." Edward waved a hand to usher him toward the doorway. "Let's saddle up."

Pecos nodded, but he first crouched down in front of the sofa where Meg reclined. "When I return from town, there's a place on the mountain I'd like to show you. A safe place," he added, knowing he alone could protect her until the current dangers snowballing her way were resolved. She wasn't the first person he'd sheltered on his land. In fact, he was highly skilled at helping innocent people disappear, something he couldn't wait to prove to her.

She waved at her bandaged ankle. "For obvious reasons, I'm not doing much traveling these days."

He was well aware of that fact. However, he was undeterred from his mission to show her the possibilities his land could offer her — namely, the safety and security. "I promise to do everything in my power to minimize your discomfort." And he wouldn't need a creaky, bouncing wagon to do so. His best-trained horse possessed a fluid gait that would jar her injury far less than the Remingtons' makeshift contraption had.

She turned pink beneath the intensity of his perusal.

Since Lacey was listening, he tried to make their proposed journey into the mountains sound like an attempt at courting. "The mountain where I live will be your home soon," he reminded gently. "I confess I am anxious to show it off to you."

Her blush deepened. "Very well. I'll bundle in my warmest layers and be ready for a jaunt up the mountain when you return from town."

He reached out to lightly touch her hand. "It is a view worth seeing, I promise."

His words elicited a shy smile from her. While she was distracted, he stealthily removed the WANTED poster from her lap and tucked it inside one of the pockets of his buckskins.

"THIS SURE DOES LOOK LIKE OUR MEG." MAV PETERSON drew on his reading spectacles and gave the WANTED poster a closer look. He was standing beside the General Store's cash register, while Pecos lounged his forearms on the counter across from him. He made a tsk-ing sound and drew his bushy gray eyebrows together. "But you're right. No one who knows her would believe she did this." He tapped one sausage-like finger against the paper. "Unfortunately, this kind of money will bring all kinds of folks running. Folks who do not know her."

Pecos kept his voice low, aware of the customers milling around the store. "Do you remember who delivered the poster to your store?"

"More an' likely, it was the clerk from the sheriff's office." Mav tapped the paper again. "Pretty much anytime they receive these in the mail, they come and toss 'em on my counter. I get more traffic than any other business in town, so it only makes sense to pin 'em up in my window."

"Is this the only copy?"

Mav shrugged. "Far as I know. I'd be happy to keep my eyeballs peeled for more."

"We must destroy them."

"Rest assured I will, Chief." Mav swiftly tore the crumpled poster into dozens of pieces. Then he swept the paper off the counter into a waste can he kept on a lower shelf.

"She is innocent, Mav." Pecos cast a furtive glance over his shoulder to ensure no one had stepped in line behind him.

Mav glanced in surprise over the top of his spectacles. "Of course she is! That gal is as sweet as molasses. I reckon that's why you and half the other fellas in town are in such a hurry to marry her, eh?" He waggled his brows teasingly at Pecos. "She's awfully purty to look at, too."

It was true. Meg was so lovely that she took his breath away, but Pecos had not come to town to sing praises about her beauty. He had bigger fish to fry. "According to Mr. Redwood, there are four others vying for her hand in marriage, but I am the right man for her." The only man for her. He needed his friend to understand that.

The shop owner chuckled. "So I've heard, Chief. So I've heard. There was quite a crowd out there earlier when that sweet gal planted a kiss on ya."

"I did not see it coming," Pecos confessed, wishing she hadn't taken it upon herself to do something so rash. He preferred being invisible — the fellow most other fellows pretended not to see when he rode through town. The locals hadn't been all that welcoming of their small but growing band of Comanches in the mountains, so it was best not to draw attention to themselves. It was certainly safer that way. Meg already had a big enough target on her head. He didn't need her association with him making it any bigger.

"I wouldn't complain too loudly about it." Mav dropped his voice conspiratorially. "As it turns out, three of the hopeful grooms made a beeline for Clink Redwood's agency the moment they heard about the kiss. Tore up their contracts and demanded their money back. That ol' reprobate was fit to be tied, let me tell ya." Mav sounded so amused that Pecos could only surmise there was no love lost between the General Store owner and the town matchmaker.

"That leaves only one man in line ahead of me." He wondered if Mav knew which of the four men was continuing to pursue Meg.

"Yes, indeed. Thatcher Mills," Mav declared before Pecos could form the question. He sounded vastly entertained. "This should be interesting. A Comanche chief and a newcomer in town going head-to-head over a purty female." He grinned. "Almost makes ya want to sell tickets and settle back to watch the show."

Pecos' heart sank. Of the four men he'd been in competition with for Meg's hand in marriage, Thatcher Mills was his least favorite candidate. He was a grim-faced cowpoke who never cracked a smile and rarely spoke to anyone. His constant glower made Pecos wonder if the fellow was secretly plotting to submit his name to the authorities as a straggler needing to be rounded up and shipped to the nearest reservation.

Heaven forbid! Then again, he wasn't going to win Meg's hand by standing around and speculating about what others were thinking. He straightened to his full height of six feet and four inches. "Good talk, Mav. I'd best get moving, so you can start selling tickets to the show."

Mav stared for a moment. Then his round features relaxed. He slapped a meaty hand down on the counter, grinning like a lunatic. "Unless my ears deceive me, you just made a joke, my poker-faced friend."

Pecos kept his expression carefully schooled as he raised a hand in farewell, which only made Mav laugh harder. His roly-poly middle shook like an oversized jar of jelly.

Pecos spun on his heels and silently left the building. His moccasins didn't leave the merest of footfalls on the plank flooring, though a nail near the door gave a faint squeak from his weight.

The noonday sun was shining at full blast overhead, making him squint. Since he and Edward had ridden separate horses into town, Pecos had no need to wait for him to finish his business with the sheriff. He valiantly hoped the lawman would be willing to take a run at Clink Redwood and put an end to his unconscionable racket. The fellow was all but operating a human trafficking ring in broad daylight.

There was Thatcher Mills still to contend with, too. Pecos mulled over what he knew about the unfriendly cowboy, a man he had every intention of beating to the altar — by buying out his contract or doing whatever else it took. Regardless, that would have to wait until later. First and foremost, he needed to transport Meg Chastain to safety.

"Let's go home, Paint." He leaped astride his Mustang and dug his heels into his flanks.

The horse gave a nicker of understanding and trotted swiftly down Main Street, leaving a cloud of dust in their wake.

UNABLE TO BEAR THE STIFLING SILENCE IN THE REAR parlor while waiting for Pecos to return, Meg reached for the crutch Edward had propped against the sofa. Though Lacey had kindly promised to brew another pot of tea for them, Meg couldn't stand the thought of enduring another hour of her sympathy. Plus, she wasn't in the mood for endlessly sitting and daintily sipping on chamomile. In the past, she'd been a woman of action, a doer and a fixer, not a person who passively waited for the chips to fall where they may.

Sadly, she wouldn't be seeing much action while bound to her crutch. With a sigh, she swayed jerkily to her feet, set it beneath her arm, and hitched her way as silently as possible from the parlor. She moved down the hardwood hallway, pushed the front door open, and stepped outside onto the porch.

Better already. She gulped in air, finding it easier to breathe outside than inside. After a pause, she limped her way around the side porch, where she could gaze at the distant mountains. The tallest mountain never failed to grab her attention. It was so beautiful and majestic, so rocky and steep, so defensible.

And somewhere high on Christmas Mountain was where Chief Pecos lived. She gave an involuntary shiver of anticipation at the thought of marrying him soon, or so she hoped. If she didn't end up behind bars instead...

She tipped her face to the heavens. "God, if You can hear me up there," she murmured, "I could really use a little help down here."

It was a simple prayer, but it was one that made her smile. Sister Mary at the orphanage would've fallen into an apoplectic fit if she'd overheard Meg praying to her Heavenly Father without a priest to intercede for her. Alas, there were no priests in residence today at the Christmas Mountain Inn.

She had no idea how long she stood there, trying not to think about how much her ankle ached. The brisk wind whistling down the mountain both chilled her and took the edge off the worst of the pain in her ankle. She should probably return indoors for her cloak, but she couldn't seem to bring herself to leave the magic of the outdoors.

The pounding of horses' hooves finally roused her from her reverie. At first, all she could see was the dust being kicked up by the steed galloping her way. Then the unmistakable outline of Chief Pecos drew into view. She'd recognize those broad shoulders and proud tilt to his head anytime, anywhere.

To her surprise, he cantered right up to the side porch where she was standing.

"Come, Meg." Unsmiling, he held out one bronzed hand to her.

Knowing she was probably breaking every rule of propriety by agreeing to accompany him without a chaperone, she limped her way across the porch to the stairs. He beat her to them, leaping off his horse and striding up them to intercept her.

He hoisted her in his arms without so much as a grunt of exertion. She awkwardly held on to her crutch, wondering what to do with it.

"Leave it," he ordered quietly. "We'll come back for it later."

Nodding, she waited until he bent his knees to prop it against the porch railing. The moment she let go of it, he carried her to his horse.

Mindful of her full skirts, he seated her sideways atop his horse. Then he leaped up behind her, careful not to jostle her injured ankle. Hooking one arm firmly around her middle, he anchored her against his chest. Then the leather toe of his moccasin wrapped around the calf of her injured leg, bracing it a few inches outward so it wouldn't bump against the horse's rounded belly.

"Thank you," she murmured gratefully. As the next gust of wind overtook them, however, she was unable to hold back a shiver.

He silently shrugged out of his buckskin jacket and slid it around her shoulders, cloaking her in his warmth that still clung to the leather.

"Won't you freeze?" she protested, wondering what he was thinking.

As usual, he didn't tell her. Instead, he nudged his horse into movement. "Take us home, Paint," he commanded softly.

Paint. His horse had a name. He also possessed a smooth trot that felt a bit like gliding. Meg tried to focus on the browns, reds, and golds of the late autumn foliage, but it was difficult to think about much else besides how close she was sitting to Pecos.

And how muscular he was.

And strong.

And protective.

And utterly wonderful.

A quick glance revealed he was wearing a long-sleeved buckskin tunic beneath the jacket he'd lent her. To her relief, she couldn't feel him shivering. She hoped he was warm enough.

Time and time again she found her head spinning in his direction, so she could admire the hard angles of his face and the black silk of his hair flowing behind him.

He dipped his head closer to hers, so he could rumble in her ear. "Do you like what you see?"

"I do," she murmured breathlessly, seeing no point in denying it.

"Tell me what you're thinking."

"I was thinking about asking you what you're thinking," she confessed with a nervous chuckle.

"I am thinking about our kiss from earlier."

"Why?" She stared in confusion at him. "You barely kissed me back."

"Not because I didn't want to."

"I-I don't understand."

"We had an audience, Two Dark Moons, and now we do not." Without warning, he swooped down to press his mouth against hers.

This time, there was no doubt in her mind that his warm, hard lips moved over hers.

At her sigh of surrender, he deepened the kiss.

Meg clung to him, realizing for the first time in a long time she no longer had any desire to run. She'd finally met her perfect match. Pecos was strong and clever. He was a good man. A worthy partner. And he was hers for the taking.

Despite his talk about not being in love, his kiss revealed just how deep his feelings ran for her. She tasted admiration and respect, tenderness and devotion. A man ready to stake his claim. A man willing and capable of serving and protecting his own.

"Pecos," she murmured shakily when he finally raised his head.

"Now you are thinking of our kiss, too."

"Yes." She could think of nothing else other than the fact she was sitting on his horse — in the circle of his brawny arms, no less. It was rather hard to believe. Only a few days earlier, they'd barely been more to each other than strangers. He'd been the silent and stoic chief of the mysterious Comanches next door, delivering the inn's daily supply of milk to a mere kitchen maid. And now they had an *understanding* — the always and forever kind!

She knew with sudden certainty that it wouldn't be difficult to fall for a man like him, that she might already be falling. *Mercy me!* Without thinking, she reached up to trace the sign of the cross on her chest.

"You are a woman of faith," he noted with interest.

"Sometimes," she sighed, feeling a little embarrassed by the reminder. *I'm supposed to be.* She'd been raised to have faith. However, all the nuns at the orphanage would be shaking their fingers at her if they could see her now. "I reckon I didn't show much faith when I skedaddled out of Riverville a few months ago. What was I thinking, Pecos? Running only made me look guilty. I should have held my ground and faced what was coming. Instead, all I've done is drag my troubles with me." She made a face. "To my employers, to my new friends…to you."

He grunted. "Your troubles brought you to me. We will face them together. Right here." He pointed at the stalwart ridges rising in front of them.

She followed the direction of his finger and found herself gazing at the foothills of Christmas Mountain. They dipped, rolled, and sliced their way clean across the horizon.

This was his home.

The sun was glinting off the rocky outsets and ledges, and there was no obvious path like the one that ran through the main village a few miles back. Out here things were less certain and less settled — mile after mile of craggy, rugged wilderness. A body could easily become lost without a proper guide to show them the way.

"Nobody knows these mountains like I do." His voice was low with conviction. "Out here you will be safe from the bounty hunters."

Meg glanced up at her groom-to-be, realizing she would additionally be wholly and completely at a man's mercy again, that she could just as easily disappear amidst these foothills and never be seen again. For a moment, a different face wavered into her mind's eye, one she had once trusted as much as she now trusted Pecos. However, she knew it wasn't fair to compare the two men.

Pecos wasn't Jones Storm, a man she'd once loved like a brother. Pecos hadn't robbed a bank and wasn't in need of someone to pin his growing list of crimes on. He simply wanted to marry her. But why?

She suddenly wanted to know. She *needed* to know.

"Why?" she blurted. "Why do you want to marry me?"

"I think you already know the answer to that," he answered easily.

"Tell me anyway," she pleaded.

There was a long pause before he started to speak again. "I have always prided myself on being independent. I live off the land and take care of my people. I train horses, and I am content. But lately, I have also been lonely." His eyes darkened with emotion. "It says in the Good Book that man was not meant to live alone. Not even Comanche chiefs." He met her gaze squarely. "So I prayed for the good Lord to send me a wife. A few days later, you stepped off the train."

His words both surprised and thrilled her. How lovely to be told she was an answer to his prayers! "You are a person of faith, too." She'd originally speculated he was a traditional Native, worshipping the sun god and such. What a relief to discover they shared some common ground when it came to the values she chose to live by.

"I am. My mother, may she rest in peace, made sure of it. She thought if she taught me to speak English and raised me as a Christian that I would have a better chance of surviving in the white man's world." His tone grew sardonic. "I am not sure she would approve of the life I've chosen for myself here in the mountains, but it is the right place for me and my people."

It was the second time he'd referenced his tribe. Meg eagerly pounced on the information. "Do you have kin here on Christmas Mountain?"

"No. I am the last of my namesake. I was referring to my fellow Comanches."

The last of your namesake? She felt her cheeks heat as the implications of his words sank in. "I reckon that means you'll be wanting to have a family?" *With me.*

"In time." The hard lines of his face didn't change. "Lord willing and you're willing."

A sense of warmth and wonder rushed over her, filling all the worried, empty spaces inside. If she was being perfectly honest, Pecos wasn't the only person who'd been lonely lately. Maybe that was partly why she'd been foolish enough to sign a mail-order bride contract. She wasn't simply running away from her troubles. Like him, she'd been searching for someone or something more. A home. A family. A place to belong and a person to belong to.

On impulse, she raised her hands to gently cup his cheeks. "I am honored to be the answer to your prayers." She leaned in to lightly brush her mouth against his.

His arms tightened around her, pulling her closer as he kissed her back.

Meg gave a soft sigh, reveling in his nearness and strength. It was wonderful to feel safe again. To be wanted and cherished. To no longer be running, not that running was truly an option any longer. If she'd searched the world high and low for the perfect man to marry, she'd have been hard pressed to come up with someone so honest, humble, hardworking, and appreciative as Pecos. She instinctively knew he would be loyal to her, and someday he would love her. Some day she would love him in return. It wouldn't be difficult. Lord help her, but he was going to be an easy man to love.

"Pecos!"

The distant shout of a man had her drawing back in alarm. She'd assumed they would be alone out here in the foothills. Pecos had all but promised they would be.

However, he didn't tense or reach for the pistol inside the holster slung around his hips.

"There you are, deputy." If anything, Pecos looked relieved as he shoved back his Stetson. "I was beginning to wonder what happened to our patrol."

Deputy? Patrol? Meg stared in shock at the dark-haired, bearded cowboy swaggering in their direction. He had a rifle slung across one shoulder and a lazy grin riding his ruggedly handsome features. Though he wore a fringed buckskin jacket, similar to the one Chief Pecos was wearing, he reminded her of someone else — two someones, actually. Jack and Jonah Hawling.

He came to stand directly in front of the horse where they were seated. "Howdy, ma'am." He doffed his hat at her with the joviality of a prince.

No! It can't be. Her eyes rounded as the truth came crashing down on her. She'd heard so much about this man — all the rumors and speculation, all the accusations and finger-pointing between the Remingtons and the Hawlings. It was a loud and raucous argument with no end in sight, one that had nearly split the town in half.

But there was no denying the identity of the man standing in front of her. The resemblance was too strong. He had to be Deputy Jesse Hawling, a local citizen who'd been missing for nigh on a year.

Except he wasn't truly missing.

And probably never had been, from the way he was grinning at her and Pecos.

CHAPTER 4: PLOTTING AND PLANNING

MEG

"You!" Her voice held a tremor of excitement. "I know who you are."

"Then that makes us even," the dusty cowboy drawled, "because I sure as blazes know who you are. You're the talk of the town, Miss Meg Chastain." He jammed his rifle under one arm and mockingly struck a prayerful pose with his hands pressed together beneath his chin. "Or should I refer to you as the future wife of my chief?"

"I am not your chief," Pecos retorted dryly. "You are like a cocklebur. A horrific nuisance and difficult to be rid of."

"But useful, nonetheless," Jesse retorted cheerfully. "Just for the record, Sanko and I headed off three interlopers at the nearest pass."

Meg wondered if Sanko was a member of the Comanche tribe. The name sounded Native to her.

She studied Jesse curiously as he scrubbed a hand over a well-groomed brown beard. She watched his smile disappear and his expression turn sober. "We sent them on a wild goose chase back to the main part of town. Said they were on the lookout for a man that rather interestingly meets the description of the woman I'm currently looking at. I reckon the two of you might know what this is all about?"

Meg briefly squeezed her eyelids shut. It had begun. Her past had finally caught up to her, and her biggest fears were realized. "Unfortunately, we do." She opened her eyelids and gravely met Jesse Hawling's probing look. "You said I was the talk of the town, so I'm surprised you don't already know."

He shook his head. "I was referring to your mile-long line of hopeful suitors."

If only that were the worst of her troubles! "The men you chased off are bounty hunters. They are searching for me."

His mouth tightened in concern as he yanked his gaze back to Pecos. "What does this mean for the tribe? For Iris and the baby?"

A baby! Meg caught her breath. In the time Jesse and his bride had been missing, they must have become parents.

"It means we have one more innocent person to protect," Pecos said firmly. "It also means we must be extra vigilant."

Gratitude flooded Meg's insides. He'd not hesitated to proclaim her innocence.

Jesse gave a long, low whistle as he gave Meg another once-over. This time his gaze settled on the bandage swathing her ankle. "You're hurt." He scowled in concern. "What happened?"

"I lost an argument with a cane chair," she supplied dryly. "Otherwise, I'd be long gone from town and all of my troubles with me."

Pecos' hand against her lower back stiffened. It was the only sign that he wasn't happy with her words.

Jesse's fierce expression softened as he glanced between the two of them. "Aw, now! You're in Comanche country now, Miss Chastain. I'm not sure what all you've heard about me, but I've been lying low in these mountains for the better part of a year. You can, too, if you wish."

He made it sound so simple that she longed to believe him. However, he wasn't the one with a $2500 bounty on his head.

A high-pitched whistle careened through the clearing, causing both Jesse Hawling and Chief Pecos to peer into the nearest copse of spruces.

To Meg's surprise, the former deputy lifted his fingers to his lips and warbled out a similar sound.

In response, an enormous creature stepped out from behind the shelter of greenery. She immediately recognized Jesse's oldest brother, Jonah. A broader version of Jesse, he was a skilled furniture maker and hunter. However, he was also known for his short fuse when he was angered. Meg had overheard many tales about his past shooting matches with Pecos and his tribe.

Like Jesse, Jonah was wearing a fringed buckskin coat. Unlike Jesse, however, he wasn't sporting a Stetson. Instead, he had a raccoon skin cap mashed atop his longish brown, wavy hair. The striped tail draped down the side of his head, tucked neatly behind one ear. He was strapped to the hilt with weaponry, too.

Meg counted two pistols in his holsters, a rifle resting against his shoulder, and a blade handle rising from one boot. Good gracious! He was prepared for any sign of trouble and then some.

"We need to talk." Jonah eyed her with interest, though she could detect no hostility in him. He angled his head, beckoning them to follow him. "It's urgent."

Pecos and Jesse exchanged a shuttered look.

"I'll alert Sanko. He'll take over the patrol while I'm away." Without any further ado, Jesse loped into the tree line.

Pecos dug in his heels to urge Paint forward. The horse settled into a near-silent walk behind Jonah. They traveled a good mile in silence, maybe longer, before they approached a homestead.

Meg had never seen the place, but she'd heard of it. It had once belonged to an ancient farmer whom everyone had simply referred to as Old Man Crocker. He had no family when he'd died a year or so ago, so he'd left the whole kit and caboodle to the Hawling brothers.

She studied the rectangular two-story house with white-washed wooden siding and pine shutters. It was a simple home, unadorned by flowers, rugs, or other feminine frills. However, it looked to be in good repair, from its sturdy front stairs to its freshly stained railings. No doubt Jonah Hawling had a hand in all the beveled rail slats and railing caps.

Pecos leaped down from his Mustang and produced a rope to tether the creature to the iron hitching post mounted to the left of the porch. He patted the horse's head and leaned closer to speak quietly to him. "I know you don't like being on a rope, old boy, but I promise I won't leave you here for long." Then he reached for Meg.

Feeling self-conscious about their audience, she placed her hands on his steely shoulders, loving the way his muscles flexed and bunched beneath her hands. He easily lifted her from his horse and hoisted her in his arms.

The move brought them face-to-face again. She scanned his stoic features, stifling the urge to lean in and kiss him again. They weren't wed, so he wasn't yet hers to kiss any time she wanted.

"How is your ankle holding up?" Though they were discussing her injury, his dark gaze dropped to her mouth.

"The ride was mercifully gentle on it," she assured. "Thanks to the crick you probably have in your foot."

"I am fine," he retorted in a scoffing tone.

"You're probably freezing."

"Not true."

The wind whipped at his long, black hair, sending a swatch of it across his eyes. Ignoring it, he marched determinedly with her up the stairs.

After a moment of hesitation, she reached up to tuck the wayward strands of hair back behind his ear.

"Thank you," he said simply.

"It's the least I can do. Your hands are full."

"That they are." He kissed her with his coal eyes, making her face heat up again.

They entered a living room that was packed with odds and ends of furniture, most of it very old-looking. There was a threadbare navy sofa on one side of the room; it was half-covered with heirloom quilts. A round glass curio cabinet rested beside it, crammed with glassware, vases, and bits of pottery. A stuffed fox with an unblinking stare kept vigil atop the curio.

Meg glanced away, knowing she'd probably jump out of her skin if she encountered such a predator in her home in the middle of the night. She turned her attention to the nicest feature in the room, the bookshelves. They were stuffed end-to-end with volumes, a surprising find in an old farmhouse like this. There were stories of adventure, poetry, and even a leather-bound Bible.

"If it feels like you stepped into a cave, it's because this home is full of men. Mostly bachelors." A petite blonde woman sashayed into the room. Her blue eyes were laughing, and her hair was piled in a complicated up-do that brought to mind a fairy princess. Her dress, however, was a modest gray wool, so pale it was nearly white. Bridal white.

She glided over to a cradle that Meg hadn't noticed resting in the corner of the room. "Hello, love," she cooed softly.

A tiny fist swung upward from the cradle.

The woman caught the little hand and kissed it. Then she

lifted the squirming bundle to her shoulder. "I am Iris, Jesse's wife, and this is our son, Little John."

"Oh!" Meg caught her breath at the sight of the lad's dimpled cheeks and chin. "He's so beautiful."

"Thank you." Iris buried her nose against the little fellow's cheek, nuzzling him and making soft, maternal crooning sounds.

"Beautiful?" Jesse scoffed, banging open the front door and striding into the room. "Pray assure me you did *not* just call my strapping beast of a son beautiful." He stomped across the room to tip his wife's face up to his. The kiss he gave her was infinitely tender and not at all brief. The mildly dazed sheen in his eyes when he lifted his head told Meg that he was madly and irrevocably in love with the mother of his son.

Lucky, lucky woman! Tasting envy over their demonstration of love and devotion, Meg turned her head away, which inadvertently brought her nose-to-nose with Pecos.

He was studying her with a heavy-lidded expression that made her heart race. *Oh, my lands!* The room seemed suddenly overfilled with babies, kisses, and emotions too complicated to name.

To her relief, Pecos gently lowered her to the navy sofa and propped her bandaged ankle atop one of the blankets.

Jonah awkwardly cleared his throat. "If you're done slurping on your wife over there, Jess...?"

"Never." Jesse adopted the stance of a boxer and feigned a few air punches in his oldest brother's direction.

Jonah ignored him and strode to the stacked stone fireplace against the outer wall of the room. He glanced in askance in Pecos' direction. "Can we speak freely?" He nodded at Meg.

"I trust her with my life." Pecos dropped a possessive hand on her shoulder, sending a delicious thrill through her.

Jonah gave her one last searching look and started to speak. "As my brothers are aware, this is where the deed to our farm has been stored ever since we inherited the property." He tapped two large fingers against one of the stones resting directly above the fireplace opening.

It was loose. He pulled it out to reveal a yawning, stone-sized opening. Thrusting his large hand inside, he pulled it back and snapped his fingers. Nothing but a drizzle of dust dropped to the floor. "As you can see, it is missing."

Jesse strode across the room to join him in front of the fireplace. "Of all the bloody —"

"Language, sweetheart!" His wife pretended to cover Little John's ears. The babe cooed something back, delighted to have his mama's full attention.

"My apologies." Jesse bent to peer inside the dark cavern.

Despite the gravity of the situation, Meg smiled. She might be a former bounty hunter and she might be tough, but she was — first and foremost — a woman, one who was drinking in every adorable sound Jesse and Iris's baby was making.

She felt Pecos' gaze on her again, but she didn't mind. Since he'd made it clear he wanted a family of his own, what could it hurt for him to witness her longing for children? It was a secret she'd held tightly to her chest for years. She'd never discussed it with anyone else, but the desire was there. It had always been there.

"Where in tarnation is the deed?" Jesse blustered, straightening to his full height.

"I don't know. It was there the last time I checked." Jonah shook his head in puzzlement. "Jack has been baking food and sneaking it over to the inn the past few days to help out while Meg is recuperating. That's where he is now, so I haven't had the chance to ask him."

"Ask me what?" The tall, wiry man in question stepped

into the room from the arched doorway leading deeper into the house. Two half doors swung into place behind him. From the delicious scents waffling through the opening above them, Meg could only surmise that the kitchen was located in the room beyond.

Jonah didn't waste any time with small talk. "Did you move the deed to the farmhouse from the fireplace?"

"A big, solid no to that." Jack playfully pointed a finger at his older brother. "Why do you ask?"

"It's missing." Jonah gestured with both hands at the empty cavern.

"When was the last time you saw it?" Jesse spun around to face those gathered. "When was the last time any of us laid eyes on it?"

The brothers spent the next minute or two muttering amongst themselves, leaving Meg to wonder why it had never occurred to them to relocate such a sensitive document to the bank vault.

"So none of us has seen it since the day we moved in?" Jonah shoved the stone back into its slot, leaving it sticking out about a half inch instead of pushing it flush against the other stones. Meg shot a knowing glance at Pecos. If Jonah had so carelessly placed it the last time he'd examined the house deed, literally anyone who'd passed through the room might've noticed and stumbled their way across the secret compartment beneath it.

Jesse began to pace back and forth in front of the fireplace. "Who else knew the deed was stored here?"

Jonah shrugged. "Edward Remington did. As a matter of fact, he was the only person in the room when Old Man Crocker was dictating his last will and testament."

The brothers stared at each other, their gazes narrowing. Meg was aghast at how quickly their suspicions had been aroused on the innkeeper's behalf. Edward was such a kindhearted man, always lending a hand to his fellow citizens. Why, he was the last person she would've suspected of wrongdoing!

"Who else, besides Edward, has visited your home since you moved in?" she inquired softly, hoping to give them someone else to point a finger at.

"Does it matter?" Jesse fisted his hands at his sides. "Edward Remington is our top suspect. The man has been buying up land right and left. It only makes sense he'd want to get his hands on this acreage as well."

"It actually doesn't make sense," she protested. "In all the months I've worked for him, he's never mistreated a soul. He's generous to a fault." She'd witnessed him giving the coat off his back to a drifter traveling through town a few weeks ago. There simply *had* to be other suspects for the Hawlings' missing home deed. There were countless other explanations that did not involve accusing Edward Remington of wrongdoing.

Watching her closely, Jack waved a hand. "Iris, Mav, the sheriff, and a good dozen or more other folks came to pay their respects to Old Man Crocker." He angled his head toward the rear of the farmhouse. "We laid him to rest under an old oak tree out back, just like he asked."

"Make a list of names," she advised. "That's how I would've tackled a problem like this back in my bounty hunting days. We'll work our way through your list one person at a time, using good ol' investigative techniques. I'll help," she offered, glancing wryly down at her injured limb, unsure of how much she could realistically do in her hobbled state. However, her job at the inn had allowed her to meet a good number of the men living on Christmas Mountain, men who'd been all too happy to talk about their lives to a willing set of ears. It was possible she would remember something that would prove useful.

"You have your own battles to fight now, Meg." Pecos gave her a sharp, searching look.

"So do you," Jesse retorted so testily that both Meg and Pecos stared at him in surprise.

Pecos grunted. "I eliminated three out of four competitors already. There's one last cowboy I have to discourage from pursuing Meg. Then we will be free to wed."

Jesse's scowl only deepened. "Is it someone I know?"

"You tell me. His name is Thatcher Mills," Pecos supplied.

"Thatcher Mills, eh?" Jesse's upper lip curled. "You do realize you're dealing with a federal marshal working undercover. Right, Chief?"

"No, I did not." Pecos folded his arms. "Why would a federal marshal sign a mail-order bride contract?"

Jonah snorted. He was still fiddling with the loose stone at the fireplace. "To marry himself a pretty woman. Why else? Marshals are still men beneath their badges, you know." The look he cast Meg held no small amount of male admiration, a stark reminder that he was a lonely bachelor himself.

"Why else?" Meg pressed a hand to her heart, feeling faint. "He might very well have been sent to town to investigate me, that's what!" What a horrible time to be dragging a broken limb around! She should've left town days ago.

"Or me!" Iris gasped from the far corner of the room. She hugged Little John so tightly that he gave a whimper of protest. She immediately gentled her hold on him. "My precious baby," she murmured against his temple. "I will *not* let any bad hombres come take your mama away from you. No, sir!"

Catching Meg's startled glance, she hastily explained, "It's a long story. The short version is, I'm an heiress with an evil guardian who'd like to slap me in an asylum, so he can take all my money."

"Money she hasn't touched in over a year," her husband

added, "so he and his thug attorney cannot trace her whereabouts."

"I see," Meg murmured. *My lands!* So that was why he and Iris had pretended to flee town. Like her, they were dodging a dangerous enemy.

"An attorney," Jesse Hawling interjected coldly, "who just so happens to be Edward Remington's father."

Meg slowly leaned back against the sofa, feeling deflated. Well, that certainly explained a lot. No wonder the Hawling brothers were at such odds with Edward Remington. His own father was part of the reason Jesse and Iris were in hiding. What a pickle! No matter what a dirty dog Mr. Remington, Senior was, however, it still didn't make Edward less of a good man.

"I don't believe Edward and his father are close," she mused aloud. "It was something his wife said that led me to that conclusion."

"They are estranged," Iris affirmed mildly. "That I can vouch for. They were at odds long before Edward left the east coast."

Jesse snorted. "Well, bully for him! The fact that he doesn't get along with his father in no way makes him a saint."

"Nor does a missing home deed make him guilty," Meg reminded quietly. "An accusation alone doesn't make a person guilty." Her own life was proof enough of that.

Jesse rounded on her. "I know everyone thinks your employer is a fine, upstanding citizen, but he's far from the do-gooder he pretends to be. Trust me."

"Easy there, deputy." His brother, Jack, stepped between them, stretching out his hands as if to hold them apart. "We're all on the same team here."

Jesse slapped aside his brother's arm and strode around him to face Meg. "Are we? Because I just today found out that the Comanche land is going up for auction, and Edward Remington intends to bid on it. That's right on the heels of buying out the sawmill, and now the deed to our farm is missing. A coincidence? I think not. He's on a mission to finish what his late grandfather started all those years ago."

"To do what, exactly?" Meg wrinkled her forehead at him. She'd been in town long enough to pick up on the fact that there was bad blood between the Remingtons and Hawlings, but this was taking things a little too far without just provocation.

"To acquire every square inch of this mountain, that's what." His chin jutted. "And just like our father got in his grandfather's way, we're in Edward's way. You." He pointed at Pecos. "Me, Jonah, and Jack. We're all in his way."

Pecos unfolded his arms and lowered them to his sides. "What's this about an auction? I assure you my land is not for sale."

"That's not what I heard," Jesse snarled. "What? Is there a deed problem with your property, as well? Because that would be all too convenient for the likes of Edward Remington!"

"No. I own all three hundred acres of my property free and clear. It was a wedding gift to my father from my mother's side of the family. He willed it to me when he passed."

Meg gaped in awe at the man she was about to marry. Because of his simple buckskin apparel, she'd assumed he was poor like herself. She couldn't have been more wrong.

Though Jesse looked as surprised as Meg felt, he was undeterred in his efforts to cast Edward Remington's character into the shadows. "Any chance you've put your eyes on your deed recently, Chief?" he inquired sarcastically. "If it's missing like ours, then we'll know exactly who's behind that auction nonsense."

It seemed to Meg that Pecos' features were flintier than

usual. He moved silently across the room and squatted in front of the sofa. "It is time for us to leave."

She nodded and reached for his shoulders without saying a word. He lifted her effortlessly into his arms and stood. Tugging his fringed jacket more tightly around her shoulders, she inwardly braced herself for their return outside into the cold.

"Aw, did I offend you?" Jesse mocked.

"No, but you've raised an issue I need to address."

Jesse scowled at the two of them. "It's probably not what you want to hear, but I'd tread carefully around the Remingtons right now. Ol' Edward has solidly wormed his way into the hearts of most of the locals. And, yes, he's a friendly enough fellow. But he was born with a silver spoon in his mouth, so his interests do not align with ours. Never did. Never will. Trust him and his ilk at your own risk."

Meg could feel Pecos' shoulders stiffen beneath her hands.

Jonah nodded, looking sad. "It does seem that every time the path of a Hawling crosses the path of a Remington, it blows up in our faces."

Jack's aquiline features wrinkled in concern. "I don't want to believe anything bad about Edward and Lacey Remington, considering how kind they've been to us, but Jesse is right. It's probably best to keep our guard up." He met Pecos' gaze. "Jesse, Iris, and the baby have been utterly dependent on the solitude of your mountains and forests this past year to keep them safe. If Edward unwittingly takes that away from us, we're going to have to come up with a new plan to protect our family."

"No man is taking my land from me." With an irritated grunt, Pecos crossed the room with Meg in his arms, making it clear they were departing.

Jack jogged ahead of them to open the front door. "Be

careful. Heaven only knows how many more bounty hunters are out there combing the woods for her."

"We will." Pecos carried her outside. The moment he and Meg were mounted on his horse, he wheeled around and headed with her into the trees. "I need to speak with Edward Remington," he notified her quietly. "Today."

She sighed, sliding her arms around his middle. "It's a pity there's so much bad blood between him and the Hawlings, when they're all such good people. I wish things could be different."

Pecos was silent for a moment. "In all of my dealings with Edward, he's been a straight shooter. There must be a reason he didn't mention the auction to me before now."

She raised and lowered her shoulders. "Maybe there's no truth to it."

His jaw tightened. "I would like to think so, but there's something afoot if Jesse says there is. He's always been a straight shooter, as well."

A volley of distant gunfire ricocheted off the mountains, sending a trickle of pebbles down the side of the nearest canyon. Meg shivered at the realization that there might be more bounty hunters out there.

Pecos dug his knees into his horse's sides to increase their speed. However, his foot remained unerringly curled around the inside of her calf, keeping her ankle from being jostled against the horse's flanks.

To her relief, the gunfire faded as they rode deeper into the foothills. Soon the faint scent of smoke swirled enticingly around their noses. It was joined by the delicious aroma of autumn stew. Venison, if Meg had to venture a guess.

When Pecos steered them into a clearing, she was amazed to discover they were on the rim of a canyon overlooking the vast wilderness below. They'd ridden due south, so they were facing the opposite direction from where Christmas Mountain Inn stood.

To their left was the steep wall of a mountain. To their right and backs was the thick forest of spruces, pines, and junipers. Scattered throughout the clearing were grazing Mustangs — one black, four red, and two dappled ones. Meg had heard that Pecos and his men captured and trained wild Mustangs, and these horses were proof of it. Was this where he kept them hidden until he was ready to market them to the villagers?

Catching her breath at the raw and wild beauty of the scene unfolding before her, she wondered why Pecos had brought her to such a remote place. Then the landscape shivered with movement as, one by one, buckskin-clad men stepped out of hiding. She counted five, then six, then seven, and still they kept coming. They wore their inky hair long like Pecos. It wasn't easy to determine their ages, only that they varied from gray heads to the more youthful countenance of a teenage lad in braids.

The details finally clicked into place as she gazed at the growing huddle of men. This wasn't simply a remote pasture for horses. Though there were no man-made structures to step inside, no fences to mark the boundaries, and no household appliances to offer comfort, he and his tribe had been living here the same way their ancestors had lived.

To the average person, it might look like an unsettled strip of land, but this was Pecos' home.

CHAPTER 5: DODGING BULLETS

PECOS

"This is where my people live." Mindful of their audience, Pecos resisted the urge to lean forward and press a kiss to the fair cheek of his affianced. "If you agree to stay with us, you will be safe here."

"Here?" He felt as much as heard the weary sigh run through her. "Please don't misunderstand me, Pecos. I'm not too proud to throw my bedroll beneath the stars. Back in my bounty hunting days, I probably slept outside more than inside, but now that I'm crippled..." Her voice dwindled uncertainly.

"I agree it is not wise for you to sleep outside, Two Dark Moons. Not with so many enemies lurking in these woods." He kept his voice low enough so only she could hear him. From the smirk Night Flyer threw his way, he doubted that he succeeded.

He swaggered up to them. "Took you a while to get back from today's milk run, eh, Chief?" The sixteen-year-old made a big show of craning his neck from one side of the horse to the other. "I reckon you forgot to bring back the empty pails." His long black braids swung through the air with his movements.

"And I reckon you forgot your manners," Pecos retorted, feeling his lips twitch. Though he would never admit it aloud, he liked the fact that the motherless nephew of his top horse trainer felt comfortable enough around him to be a tease. Heaven knew he had endured more than his share of heartache in recent years. It was good to see the lad happy again.

Unlike the other seventeen Comanches living in the mountains with Pecos, Night Flyer preferred to wear cowboy boots. He was growing up with an interesting mixture of Native American mannerisms with a Texan flair. Pecos wished he could talk the lad's uncle, Sanko, into sending Night Flyer into town a few days per week to study with a tutor, but so far his suggestion had been met with stubborn silence. Perhaps when Pecos and Two Dark Moons were wed, Sanko would be willing to let her teach the boy to read.

Night Flyer's sun-kissed features adopted a sly expression. "I hope you weren't expectin' me to act all mannerly with the strangers in the pass earlier."

A silent warning gonged inside Pecos's chest. "What strangers?"

"Never saw 'em before." Night Flyer shrugged. "If I had to guess, I'd say they were out-of-towners with their fancy pants and boots. But don't worry. I shot an arrow at the trap we set and sent a rockslide down on 'em. You shoulda seen em' yellin' and shootin' in the air."

Pecos felt his blood turn cold. "Let us pray they did not see your arrow." Any reports of Natives shooting at settlers could send the wrath of the Texas Rangers down on them.

"They didn't, Chief." Night Flyer shot him a scoffing grin. "I shot it straight into the cord wrapped around the bush, just like you showed me. It held fast while the pebbles rained down."

"And did you think to go fetch your arrow after they left?"

"I did, sir." Night Flyer reached inside the quiver hanging over his shoulder and produced the arrow in question. "The tip broke off, so I had to replace it." He waved the freshly repaired arrow in the air at them.

"Good job." Pecos was impressed at the lad's ingenuity, though he was less than thrilled about the appearance of two sets of bounty hunters in the same afternoon. "I have another assignment for you." He glanced tenderly down at the lovely woman riding in front of him on his Mustang. "Pray give Miss Chastain a tour of her guest chambers, while I pay a visit to Edward Remington."

Night Flyer snapped to attention like a soldier, "I'd be happy to, Chief."

Pecos leaped to the ground and landed in silence on the balls of his feet. Then he stretched his arms out to Meg.

"I think you're forgetting something," she warned softly. "My crutch is back at the inn."

"As promised, I will bring it when I return." He adored the trusting way she pressed her hands on his shoulders for leverage and leaned into him as he lifted her down. He wanted to kiss her goodbye but did not wish to embarrass her in front of his comrades. Despite his reluctance to let her go, he swiftly transferred her to Night Flyer's arms. "Would you like me to fetch anything else for you from the inn?"

She looked perplexed. "You truly intend for me to spend the night out here?"

"No." He angled his head at the hidden caverns in the mountain wall beyond them. "Night Flyer will show you to your chamber."

"My chamber?" She glanced in askance around them.

Pecos nodded at Night Flyer, who spun with her in his wiry arms and headed for the caverns.

Sanko limped to his side and patted Paint's neck. He was a rangy Native in his early forties, a man who'd lost his wife to a fever and his two sons to a shoot-out with the Rangers. It had happened nearly three years ago — the day his entire village had been rounded up for transport to the nearest reservation. He and his nephew were the only ones who'd escaped during the melee.

"I will see to your horse." He gave a sharp whistle and a fresh mount came running up to them, a black Mustang they'd aptly named Midnight. "This one would enjoy a bit of exercise. I haven't had the time to put him through all of his paces yet today."

Pecos leaped astride the fresh horse. "I was hoping your minister friend in the next town over might be willing to marry us." He angled his head in the direction Meg was retreating.

Sanko's dark brows rose a smidgeon. "I thought you were signing one of those new-fangled mail-order bride contracts."

"That was my original plan." Pecos leaned forward to smooth a hand down the horse's neck. He was a jumpy stallion, pawing at the ground to be off. "However, the town matchmaker doesn't seem too anxious to do business with a Comanche, so my plans have changed."

Sanko shook his dark hair to one side as he glanced over his shoulder at Meg. "Is she willing?"

"Yes." Pecos could still taste the sweetness of her kisses on his lips.

"You better be sure."

"I am."

"Then I'll send word to my friend." Sanko made a snorting sound and let go of his hold on Midnight's mane.

Midnight pawed at the ground again and took off at a

trot. When they reached the tree line, he slowed down somewhat. Every time they reached a clearing, however, he broke into a run again.

Pecos let him fly like the mountain breeze. Sure, he was in the business of capturing and gentling the wild Mustangs. He first saddle broke the ones he sold to the villagers. However, no amount of training could ever fully erase from their memories what it had felt like to freely roam these mountains. So, now and then, he gave them another taste of it.

In less than ten minutes, the rooftop of Christmas Mountain Inn drew into view. He pulled on Midnight's mane to signal to him that it was time to slow down. Stopping just inside the copse of trees, Pecos took a moment to survey the rear grounds of the inn.

Dry grasses blew in the late autumn breeze. A jackrabbit shot across the lawn and disappeared beneath a newly erected gazebo. This time of day, a caribou or two could usually be spotted grazing through, but not today. A trio of horses Pecos wasn't familiar with were tied to the hitching post, and a cacophony of male voices rose from the direction of the front veranda.

They were voices Pecos didn't recognize, loud and angry voices. Gritting his teeth, he swung down from his horse and led him to the hollowed-out tree where he occasionally stored supplies. Not too long ago, he'd tucked a regular shirt and trousers inside the tree, along with a Stetson. He'd learned that sometimes it was best to hide his Comanche roots and fade into the townsfolk.

He wasted no time changing, loosely braiding his hair and stuffing it inside his hat. Other than the fact his jaw was as smooth as silk, with no hint of an evening shadow, he could easily pass for a villager in his faded denim trousers and boots.

Since he'd ridden Midnight back, he gave the creature the

command to remain in the woods. With a short nicker of protest, Midnight bent his head to snatch up a mouthful of dry grass. He tilted his dark head and stared belligerently at Pecos as he chewed.

"I'll take you for another run soon," Pecos promised, amused by the horse's cocky antics.

Midnight bobbed his head before dropping it to take another bite of grass, which made it look as if he was nodding in agreement.

Pecos left him to stride across the empty lawn and skip up the back porch stairs of the inn. Like the front veranda, a row of painted rockers graced the back porch. There were six of them in all, stretching across the plank floor.

He lifted his fist and gave a tentative knock, three quick raps the way he did when delivering milk each morning. To his surprise, the door opened before he could finish his last knock.

Lacey faced him, looking so distraught that his heart wrenched with sympathy. Her lovely blue eyes were red-rimmed as if she'd been weeping. "Er, Pecos?" A slow smile tugged at her lips as she peered closer at him. "Is it really you?" She was clutching her chubby nephew, Malachi, whom she and Edward had adopted a while back.

"Yes, ma'am." He leaned in to chuck the lad under the chin, surprised that Lacey was still toting him around on her hip like a sack of potatoes. The child was plenty old enough to walk.

"Come inside," she hissed, glancing furtively around the back yard as she waved him forward.

"Is everything alright?" He held out his arms, offering to take the lad from her, but she shook her head.

"Not exactly." She glanced around his shoulder one last time before shutting the door. "Where is Meg?"

"Safe," he answered cryptically, not yet ready to divulge her location.

"Good." Thankfully, Lacey didn't pry. "As you can imagine, we've had bounty hunters traipsing in and out of here all afternoon." She gave Malachi a reassuring squeeze.

"I was afraid of that," Pecos muttered. Though he was sorry to hear it, it served as affirmation that he'd gotten Meg away from the inn in the nick of time.

"The things they're accusing her of," Lacey stormed, looking indignant. "Everything from stealing their dinners to making babies cry. As if!" she huffed. "Malachi adores her to pieces. I've never had to endure listening to so much nonsense in all my life."

Normally, Pecos would've removed his hat once he stepped inside, but the length of his hair would give away his Comanche heritage to any onlookers. To his relief, he appeared to be alone with Lacey and Malachi.

She led him to the same private parlor in the rear of the building where they'd last visited. "It's not safe for you outside right now I'm afraid, even dressed as you are."

"Why not?" He moved to stand in front of one of the bookcases, contemplatively folding his arms.

She looked genuinely distressed. "Word is spreading like wildfire about the way you kissed Meg in full view of everybody."

Pecos snorted in derision. Meg had kissed *him*, not the other way around, but he saw no reason to argue the point.

"They assume you know her whereabouts, and Heaven only knows what some of them might do to drag the information from you."

"So they're combing the countryside for both of us," Pecos mused bitterly. *That figures*. More than likely, the men searching for them would presume they were criminals without ever giving them the chance to defend themselves.

Alas, the bronze color of his skin would only further fuel their suspicions.

"They are. They're fussing up a storm about it, too." She squatted down to place Malachi on a quilt on the floor. A small stack of toys was piled on one end of it. He pounced on them with a crow of delight. "Apparently, the Hawling brothers have been shooting over the heads of anyone who trespasses on their land. The last group had a fellow whose hat got shot off." She gave a chortle of unholy glee.

Shoving a handful of red-gold curls from her face, she fixed a friendly smile on Pecos. "I'm presuming you came to have a word with Edward, but I don't know how long he'll be tied up with that latest batch of scallawags out front. Would you care for some tea while you wait?"

Pecos was about to turn down her generous offer, but his stomach chose that moment to rumble in hunger. Loudly.

Lacey wrinkled her nose at him. "I think I have my answer." She waved him toward the sofa and chairs in the gathering area of the room. "Sit and keep an eye on Malachi for me. I'll be right back."

He remained standing, though he nodded respectfully at her as she swished past him in her lacy gown that matched Meg's. It was a reminder of the Remington's generosity and strengthened his convictions that he was right to come beg a word with Edward.

It was way too bad about all the bad blood between him and the Hawlings. Pecos had heard more than his fill of it during the past year, and it still made little sense. All he could gather was that Edward's grandfather and Jesse's father had been friends who pretended not to be friends in order to protect a woman from going to jail. Apparently, the late Mrs. Hawling had taken the law into her own hands and shot and killed a man who'd attacked her. It was a sad tale with an unfortunate twist that involved Mr. Hawling confessing to a crime he hadn't committed. He was currently serving out a life sentence to protect his wife's reputation and his sons' good memories of her.

The feud between the Remingtons and Hawlings had grown out of that same tale, with the townsfolk taking sides and adding fuel to the rumors. Pecos had never given the rumors much credence, presuming there were as many untruths as truths mixed in with them by now. However, the missing deed to Hawlings' farmhouse and the talk of auctioning off Pecos' land, had him wondering exactly where Edward stood on all this.

Lacey reappeared with tea and a tray of dainty little cakes. Pecos thanked her for her kindness and ate like he was famished. He still had to wait nearly a full hour before Edward stomped inside the parlor to join him.

He looked uncharacteristically windblown and harried. His black leather boots, which were normally polished to a glassy shine, were covered in a layer of fine dust; and his hat was jammed carelessly under one arm. "I'm not sure about the wisdom of meeting with our next guest inside...oh!" He stopped short at the sight of Pecos. "Hello, Pecos." His relief was palpable.

Since Edward appeared to be alone, Pecos finally took off his hat. His braid slid out to dangle down his back. "Edward." He inclined his head.

Edward made a sound of exasperation. "Though I'm glad to see you're in good health, the other part of me wishes you hadn't ventured into town. Not this evening, at any rate." He eyed Pecos' change of clothing with interest. "Well, I'll be! The jeans and boots are a mighty clever idea."

"I thought so." Again, Pecos politely inclined his head.

"Still, it's risky coming all the way here. Why did you?" Edward accepted the teacup his wife offered him. He blew at the steam rising from it while he waited for Pecos to respond.

Though he tossed his hat on a nearby chair, he didn't remove his black overcoat.

Wanting to watch the innkeeper's reaction, Pecos launched straight into his main reason for visiting. "I want to know about the land auction."

Edward grimaced and looked away. "I've been meaning to have a talk with you about that."

"So it's true." It looked as if Jesse's warning hadn't been that far off the mark, after all. "You have your eye on my property." If that was the case, there was one big, looming problem with the man's plan. It wasn't for sale. The sooner Edward accepted that fact, the better for them both.

Edward looked uncomfortable. "There's been talk about filing a petition to nullify your deed."

Pecos' blood raced hotly. "On what grounds?"

"Do you really have to ask?" Edward turned back to meet his gaze.

"My mother was white, and my name is on the deed."

"Well, a few unscrupulous folks are claiming you're harboring Natives who should've been relocated to reservations long ago. They've not gone so far as to claim you're amassing weapons or planning to mount an attack against the U.S. Government, but you know what'll happen if they do."

Pecos' insides felt cold. "My people live, train, and sell horses there. Nothing more." As far as he was concerned, he had every right to invite whomever he wanted to live there. "Like me, several of them are half white." Night Flyer was one of them.

"I am aware, and I've made that same statement to anyone who will listen. Methinks it would be easier for me to convince them if they could see you dressed as you are now." Edward surveyed him critically. "It would also help if you built an actual house on your property and showed signs of acclimating into the community." He waved his hands, presumably to take in the mountains and canyons.

"Might I ask who *they* are?" Anger rolled through Pecos, though he held it in check.

"A band of out-of-town investors that I have reason to believe are being represented by none other than my father." Edward's mouth twisted as if he was tasting something bitter. "Which means you're not their only target."

Pecos gave the innkeeper a hard, searching look and read nothing but raw honesty in his features. "So they wish me to dress like a white man and live like a white man," he noted dryly. "Otherwise, your attorney father and his cronies are going to petition away my rights to own my land?"

"They can try. I'm not saying they'll win in court. Our judge is a good man. Plus, we currently have a mayor in office who is easily swayed by generous donations. To be frank, greasing his hand with a little gold might be the quickest way to put an end to all of this."

Pecos had no interest in paying bribes. Another far more palatable defense popped into his mind. "Will it help if I marry a white woman?" Though it, by no means, had ended his father's uphill battle against the prejudices directed at his heritage, it had certainly opened a lot of new doors for him in society.

Edward's weary expression relaxed in a smile. "Normally, I would say yes. A thousand times, yes! But I'm afraid our sweet little Meg comes with a whole other pack of trouble. So if there's any way of talking you out of pursuing her...?" He let the question settle between them.

"There's not." It was far too late for that. "Your wife blew into town with a pack of trouble, too, if I recall." Pecos had decided months ago that Two Dark Moons was a woman worth fighting for, down to his last breath.

Edward gave a dry chuckle. "Indeed, she did. As Mav likes to say, women are trouble."

So are men. Pecos wasn't amused. "Any idea why a federal marshal working undercover is making payments on a mail-order bride contract for Meg?"

Edward's dark brows rose. "How in tarnation did you find out about that?"

Pecos kept his expression carefully bland, though he was incensed to learn how much Edward had been keeping from him on a number of important matters. "A friend of mine recognized him."

"A friend, you say?" Edward abruptly set his teacup on the mantle. A stunned brand of joy infused his aristocratic features. "By all that is great and good, Pecos! Pray assure me this means that Jesse Hawling is alive and well!"

Pecos realized too late that he'd said too much. However, there was no slipping things past Edward Remington's attorney's mind. "I can neither confirm, nor deny what you're asking," he teased, borrowing a legal phrase he'd once heard the innkeeper use.

"Oh, give way!" Edward exploded. "After the day I've had, there's nothing that would make me happier than to discover Jesse is still in town. Or back in town. Or never left town." His gaze narrowed. "You do realize that harboring fugitives from the law will not help your land deed case."

"Then it appears I'm going to need a good lawyer to represent me." Pecos had the funds to hire Edward, but he knew the man wouldn't want that sort of payment from him. "Perhaps you could recommend someone to me?"

"Perhaps I could if you're willing to answer my question about Jesse."

"You only wish to know about Jesse?" Pecos pretended surprise. "Not about Iris or the baby?"

Edward's smile grew so wide it was a wonder his face

didn't crack. "Now that you mention it, I reckon they should've had their baby by now. Was it a boy or a girl?"

"They call him Little John."

"Ah." For a moment, Pecos thought he saw a glint of tears in his neighbor's eyes, but Edward blinked and turned away before he could be certain. He walked to the window to stare across the rear grounds of the inn property. "I don't blame him one bit for going into hiding. I would've done the same thing if I was in his shoes, and Lacey's well-being was at risk. You'll soon find there's nothing you won't do for the woman you love. Or your children." He shook his head. "Even though Malachi is adopted, it didn't take him long to wrap both of his small hands around my heart."

In that moment, Pecos' last doubts about Edward vanished. He was a man who could be trusted. All the mixed signals, misunderstandings, and nonsense that the Hawlings had allowed to get between them and their friendship wasn't worth a hill of beans. Edward Remington's father might be the Devil reincarnate, but his younger son was a good man.

"I would be honored to have you represent my case," he declared humbly. "I won't leave my land without a fight, though I'll be praying day and night it doesn't come to that." Military skirmishes never ended well for Natives on the run, and the country was fast running out of places for them to run to. "I'm even willing to build a blasted house or two, if that's what it takes to convince folks that I'm civilized enough to reside in this town." His mouth twisted bitterly. "Who knows? Maybe I can even talk some of my tribe into living in them."

Edward spun around from the window, his expression grave. "Of course I'll represent you. And please understand, the only reason I was considering bidding on your property was to keep the land the way it is. I don't want commercial builders coming in here and tearing up the place any more than you do. It was never my intention to make you leave."

"Maybe you wouldn't have." Pecos pinned him with a hard, knowing look. "But someone eventually would have. That's how ownership works. Only the man holding the deed gets to stay for good. I am that man, I hold that deed, and I need you to help me keep it."

Edward strode across the parlor to extend his hand. "I will do everything I can to help, right down to advising you to mine some of that gold from the caverns dotting our property line. I know we agreed to leave it alone for fear of destabilizing the mountain. But here's the cold, hard truth. A little money might go a long way to earn the mayor's support. He went over budget months ago when the bridge on the north pass collapsed and had to be rebuilt."

They leaned in to clasp hands, not a quick palm-to-palm shake, but hand to forearm in the Old World way. It was the kind of agreement that brought two men eye-to-eye, where each could see the true intent of the other — close enough to whip out a blade and plunge it into the other's chest, and close enough to choose not to.

"My friend." Chief Pecos inclined his head, knowing that real progress had been made in their conversation, the kind that would affect generations to come.

"My friend," Edward responded, sounding a tad choked with emotion. "Now take me to see that rascal deputy you've been harboring. I've hoped, prayed, and waited a very long time for this day."

CHAPTER 6: SURPRISING DISCOVERIES

PECOS

While Edward hurried to saddle up one of his horses in the stable, Pecos jogged to the front porch to quickly retrieve Meg's crutch. He gave a quick peek out the door before stepping outside, just to make sure the front yard was clear of uninvited guests. It was. The crutch was right where they'd left it, propped against the railing. He snatched it up and returned inside to cut through the inn, intending to depart through the rear exit.

"Wait, Pecos!" Lacey glided down the hardwood stairs as he skirted them. The ornately curved railing jutted out into the foyer.

He reluctantly paused in his march down the hallway to glance expectantly up at her. Old photographs lined the wall of the stairwell, presumably of Remington ancestors. Several were yellowed with age, which only added to their charm. An antique credenza rested against the opposite wall of the foyer. In the past, Meg had nearly always kept it stocked for the pleasure of their guests with a tray of fresh-baked tea cakes or cookies. Today, it held an array of crackers and breads with a jar of canned preserves that Pecos recognized as more of

Meg's handiwork. The former bounty hunter was truly a wizard in the kitchen.

"We miss her," Lacey confessed softly as she cleared the stairs and came to stand in front of Pecos. "I hope she gets to come back some day when the real criminal is finally caught — not as an employee, but as a friend. Until that day, however, it is up to you to keep her safe."

"I will," he promised soberly.

"I know you will, and pray deliver this to her." She removed the handle of a simple black travel bag from her shoulder and held it out to him. "Meg pretends to be an outdoorsy woman who needs nothing but her own grit to survive, but she is still a female. I assure you she will appreciate a few female things during her stay in your mountain village."

"My village?" He stared at her in surprise as he accepted the travel bag.

She nodded, looking smug. "I've gone exploring a few times, and I've never once run across a teepee city, a longhouse, or any sign of one. However, you and your people have to be living somewhere, so I kept searching until I figured out where."

"You trespassed on my property?" Swallowing a groan, Pecos looped Meg's travel bag across his chest and shoved it behind him. It would be easier to ride home with it draped across his back.

She gave a flippant shrug. "I wouldn't call it that. We're neighbors, after all. And friends, I hope."

"I never invited you onto my land," he returned mildly. It wasn't that he was trying to be unneighborly; he was merely protecting his people and their way of life.

She raised her chin. "Well, you should have. And, if you truly mean to marry our Meg, then you'd better get around to inviting me." She tossed her head. "Because I have no intention of giving up my friendship with her."

He hardly knew what to say to that.

"There aren't many womenfolk on this mountain," she reminded. "The three of us need to stick together."

"Three?" He eyed her sharply.

She nodded, blinking back happy tears. "I was eavesdropping on your conversation with Edward, too," she informed him in a tone utterly without remorse.

Her joy at knowing Iris was still in town was so obvious that Pecos didn't have the heart to maintain his silence on the topic. "Very well, my nosy neighbor. I will let both women know how anxious you are to visit them. In the meantime, however..." He lowered his voice in warning.

"I know, I know." She waved a hand impatiently at him. "I will carry your secrets to the grave, Pecos. I am stronger than I look and can be a brutally stubborn woman when my mind is made up. Just ask Edward."

In response, Pecos pressed a hand to his chest.

To his surprise, she impulsively stepped closer to throw her arms around his middle. "I have one more request. Keep my husband safe," she begged.

He patted her shoulders awkwardly, feeling no small amount of awe at the blind trust she was putting in him. In the next moment, his heart wrenched with worry as he pondered who would remain behind to keep her safe while her husband was away. "Will you be here alone?" he asked.

"Good gracious, no!" She stepped back and dropped her arms. "Edward would never allow it." She lowered her voice to barely above a whisper. "Thatcher Mills is staying here at the inn with a pair of Pinkerton detectives. I assure you that Malachi and I will be in good hands while Edward is away." Glancing furtively at the ceiling, she raised her voice to a more normal volume. "Mav from the General Store is supposed to pay us a visit, too."

The undercover marshal was on the premises, with no less than two comrades-in-arms? Why? That was news to Pecos.

Lacey gave a short laugh as she scanned his face. "Edward didn't tell you, did he?"

"I know who he is, if that is what you're asking." The part about Thatcher Mills working undercover. That was due to Jesse, though, not Edward.

"Oh, good!" She drew a deep breath and returned to the same whispery tone as before. "I can't tell you how relieved I was to find out his mail-order bride contract was merely part of his cover. If what I overheard is correct, he already has a wife, one in the family way, whom he is most anxious to return to." She beamed a merry smile up at him. "So when he finally arrests Clink Redwood, there will be absolutely no one standing in your way to wed our sweet Meg!"

Arrest him for what? Pecos would've liked to linger at the inn and learn more from Edward's chatty wife, but he needed to hit the trail before dark. Besides, he'd have Edward at his side to ply with more questions.

Gripping Meg's crutch, he nodded his farewell to Lacey. "Thank you for the tea."

"Any time, Pecos. I mean it," she called after him as he made his way down the dimly lit hallway. "We live too close to be strangers."

He exited onto the back porch and jogged across the lawn to the trees, where Midnight awaited him. The Mustang was only twenty to thirty yards from where he'd left him grazing. He raised his head, tossed his mane, and trumpeted out a greeting.

"Enough grumbling." Pecos strode up to him, unsurprised when the horse reared back on his hind legs and cycled the air. The stallion had grown up in the wilderness and wasn't yet fully acclimated to being ridden.

He was careful to maintain eye contact with the magnificent beast, neither backing up nor flinching. It was important for the horse to see his master showing strength and bravery. "My apologies for my lateness. I've come to return you to your herd." Midnight had mated with one of the wild mares, and she would be foaling soon. Pecos and his team of horse trainers had waited to bring her into the herd, not wanting to put any undo pressure on her in her current state. It seemed to him that Midnight had done a decent enough job on his own of keeping her close.

Pecos and his comrades would take the foal, of course, as soon as it was born. That was their trump card for ensuring its mother would be willing to join the herd. They'd used this technique many times before, and it hadn't failed them yet. It took more time and patience than chasing the wild Mustangs into a lather and lassoing them into submission, but it was worth the wait. It allowed his tribe to slowly build trust with the creatures, which always paid off when it came time to teach them to accept a rider.

Midnight continued to whinny and paw the air for a few moments, more for show than anything else. Then he plopped down on all fours and stepped forward to press his nose against Pecos' hand.

"Whew!" Edward rode into view at a steady walk on his Palomino. "From a distance, I could see him rearing up and wondered if you needed a hand." He gave a wry huff. "I know you've been doing it for years, but it can't be easy showing these wild Mustangs who's boss."

It wasn't something Pecos would describe as hard, either. "It's our way of life." One that would go away entirely if he and his comrades started blasting holes into the side of the mountain on some fool's errand. Not to mention all the prospectors it would flood the foothills with as soon as word got out about someone striking gold. No, there had to be a better way to solve his current dilemma — a better way than mining and bribing.

Pecos leaped astride his horse, hating that he had no time to change back into his buckskins. Midnight had not yet been saddle broken, so he was unaccustomed to the rough rasp of denim or the hard press of a boot heel. However, he was accustomed to Pecos' scent and weight. Fortunately, that proved to be enough on the short ride back to his home.

With a little luck, Jesse and his wife would be back from their visit to the family farm. Pecos wished it was safe for them to move there permanently, but the risks were still too great. His wife's unscrupulous uncle was still in charge of her fortune, a man who occasionally paid spies to nose around town and inquire into her whereabouts. Jesse was the only reason Iris remained free of the asylum where her uncle wished to incarcerate her, but that freedom had come at a cost.

Jesse and Iris had all but disappeared off the face of the earth a year earlier. The only folks who knew their where-abouts were Jonah and Jack Hawling, Pecos and his band of Comanches, and now Edward and Lacey Remington. Pecos could only hope Jesse would forgive him for bringing the Remingtons into their confidence, since Edward was the one man in the world Jesse couldn't seem to stop belly-aching about.

Pecos was hard pressed to understand the dynamics between Jesse and Edward, other than the two men seemed fated to clash. Sadly, Pecos was about to be personally respon-sible for their next clash.

It was a bit awkward riding the spirited Midnight with Meg's crutch in his hand, but he managed. Midnight showed no mercy, however. When Pecos gave him his head, he selected the steepest stretches of terrain, ofttimes only narrowly clearing the low-lying tree branches.

"He's punishing you," Edward noted dryly as they reconvened on the final rocky stretch of path leading home.

He was, but Pecos didn't mind. "Sometimes he likes to remind us how he used to soar through these passes with no man to answer to. However, he'll appreciate the feed and water Sanko and Night Flyer give him this evening." And he wouldn't put up a fuss when it came time to join the other Mustangs inside their cavern barn, safe from the cutting night winds, coyotes, and frost. The only times Midnight complained after dark was when his mate grazed close enough outside for him to sense her presence.

"Seems as if the two of you understand each other." Edward sounded impressed. He squinted at them in the deepening shadows of twilight. The trees were slowly changing from their shades of green to black silhouettes. A wolf howled in the distance, and an occasional pebble crackled down the jagged incline of the cliff walls on either side of them.

Pecos didn't answer. Horses were easy to understand. It was their human counterparts who made things complicated with their buggies, wagons, coaches, plowshares, and endless ways of restricting the beasts' freedom of movement. He'd long since lost track of the number of saddles, stirrups, bits, crops, and whips the western riders employed. Take all of those items away, and horses were simply, well...horses.

Which gave him an idea. "Earlier you mentioned raising money to repair a bridge."

"I did, but the whole point of that conversation was to put a prettier face on plain old-fashioned bribery." Edward's upper lip curled. "Greasing the hands of the powers-that-be."

Sometimes Pecos had a difficult time understanding all the complicated verbal expressions his friends employed, but he knew what bribery meant. "What if we simply raise money and give to a worthy cause? No bribery." He ducked as Midnight crashed through the underbrush, barely clearing a low-lying branch. The maneuver nearly scraped Pecos off the horse's back.

"How so?" Edward sounded dubious.

"By sponsoring a rodeo. It's something a lot of folks have been asking for. Plus we'll find out what the mayor's next big project is and donate a percentage of our profits to it."

Edward nodded. "I take it this is your way of saying no to the gold mining alternative, correct?"

"It is." Pecos would only stoop to swing a pickax as a very last resort to save his land. "My feelings on the topic have not changed." He was dead set against it. A sudden hoard of gold seekers could do irreparable damage to the mountain, plus destroy its serenity in one fell swoop. It would hardly matter if he still held the deed to the land afterward. There'd be nothing left worth having.

"I reckon it makes sense, with you being a horseman and all." Edward mulled on that for a moment. "It'll take more than one rodeo, though, to raise the kind of money we're talking about."

"I am aware." Pecos had done quite a bit of soul-searching on the topic, which was why what he was about to say next felt so right. "That's why I'm going to build rodeo facilities on my land. We can sponsor rodeos year-round. Not only will we raise money, it'll spread goodwill, provide a living for my family and friends, and compliment my Mustang business."

Edward's dark brows rose as he pondered the plan Pecos was laying out. "You're serious, aren't you?"

"I am. It's something I've been praying about, and this is what I feel I'm meant to do next."

"Go into the rodeo business, eh?"

"It makes sense."

"It actually does. Impressively so." Edward sounded amazed.

"Like Ma used to say, God always has a plan." Pecos' mind was racing with excitement over the possibilities. In his herd, he had horses for every situation — half-wild Mustangs suitable for bronc riding, fast horses that could be raced, and mares and ponies for the less adventurous. Because of his access to the herds roaming the mountains, he would have an unlimited supply of horses. Additionally, the rodeo would bring in a continuous stream of potential buyers for his Mustang business. Since the Hawling brothers served as middle men and did most of the boarding, showing, and re-homing of the Mustangs for a reasonable fee, the rodeos would mean more business for them all.

"Bringing in the rodeo crowd would impact all the businesses in town." Edward gave a low whistle. "It would keep my inn packed to overflowing. I'd probably have to expand. Not that I'm complaining. Expansion is one of those nice problems to have."

"Why hasn't someone thought of doing this before?" Pecos was surprised nothing was in the works yet, considering how many townsfolk were forever yammering about rodeos. A body could hardly step inside Mav's General Store without hearing about it.

"Oh, they've thought about it alright, but you know how it is." Edward waved a hand. "Nobody wants to shoulder that much responsibility."

Neither did Pecos. It was way too much work for one person, but he just happened to have a whole tribe of men who'd be happy to take on such a project.

Plus, times were changing. Every acre of land around them was being bought up right and left. It was only a matter of time before his people, and the wild horses they herded, would be completely boxed in by property lines. When that happened, he would still have eighteen Comanches to keep gainfully employed, and that didn't include the woman he was about to marry, any children they'd be blessed with, or the future families that would form within his tribe. He had a whole village to look after, and a rodeo business would play an integral role in making that happen.

God be with us. He offered up a silent prayer into the night. "I have seventeen able-bodied Comanches who will help me start my rodeo business. That will be our contribution to Christmas Mountain. We will host it on our land, which means we'll get to reconstruct all those buildings and fences you've been talking about to prove we're civilized." It would require his tribe to make some big changes in the way they lived. It would be a bittersweet merging of the past and the present, the old and the new. The timing was perfect, however, since Pecos was about to marry a white woman.

"I almost don't know what to say, Chief." Edward's voice was hushed with respect.

"It'll be just Pecos from now on." Within his inner circle, Pecos would still be a chief, but he didn't need the local mayor to continue viewing him as competition. "Pecos Carlson." It was the name on his property deed. It didn't have quite the same majestic ring as Chief Pecos, but times were changing.

As they drew nearer to the clearing outside of the caverns where he and his tribe lived, Pecos glimpsed the flicker of golden flames. Though it was late, his men had a bonfire going. Fifty yards or so closer, and he could hear the minor notes of a flute being played along with the rumble of drums.

Moonlight poured down on him and Edward as they rode into the center of the merriment. His gaze immediately sought out and landed on Meg. Night Flyer had her seated on a pile of bearskin blankets next to the fire. He'd also provided her with a set of buckskins. She looked warmer and infinitely more comfortable than she had in her piles of skirts and petticoats from earlier.

As he had before, Sanko trotted up to claim his mount as Pecos slid to the ground. They silently leaned in to clasp hands to forearms. Then they wordlessly parted.

Meg glanced up as Pecos approached the fire. "My crutch!" she exclaimed, reaching eagerly for it.

Pecos took a seat beside her on the furs, laying her crutch on the ground behind them. He lifted the strap of her travel bag from his shoulder next and set it atop the crutch. "I've been away for hours, and all you're concerned about is that old stick?" Shoot! He would fashion her a far nicer one on the morrow.

Her cheeks darkened in the moonlight, indicating she was blushing. Unable to resist her beauty, he leaned closer to gaze into her eyes.

Back in town, he'd felt the need to exercise utmost caution around her, so as not to offend the locals with his "savage" pursuit of the only unwed female in town. Not so on his own land with his own people. He lightly pinched her chin between his thumb and fingers, tipping her face up to his.

She caught her breath, smiling shyly at him. "Thank you for the change of clothing." She fingered the delicate beading at the neck of her tunic, which matched the beading on her leggings. Her dark, silky hair was still piled in a complicated twist atop her head. However, a bunch of tendrils were dancing against her temples and cheeks in the evening breeze.

Instead of answering, he closed the distance between them and touched his mouth to hers. Though the evening was chilly, her lips were warm and soft. Never before had he experienced such a sense of coming home.

"I missed you," he whispered against her lips.

"I missed you, too." There was a tremulous quality to her voice.

He drew back enough to drink in the beauty of her soulful eyes, enjoying the play of emotions through them. "I discovered some interesting things this evening. One of them is that the marshal's mail-order bride contract on you is merely part of his cover story. You and I are free to wed whenever you are ready." He was ready. He would wed her in a heartbeat, just as soon as she said the word.

"Er, not exactly." Edward Remington cautiously cleared his throat from somewhere nearby.

Inwardly groaning over the interruption, Pecos reluctantly swung his head to seek him out. "What now?" Though he respected the innkeeper as a friend and fellow business owner, he wouldn't have minded a little more time alone with Meg before anyone else joined their conversation.

Edward squatted down next to him and held out his hands to the flames. "It is true that Thatcher Mills is working undercover." He cast a sideways look at Meg, as if to gauge her reaction to what he was about to say. "He's building a case against Clink Redwood, and he's going to need a little more time to do so. I promised him I'd speak with you about it in the hopes of gaining your cooperation."

She shot a half-worried, half-regretful look up at Pecos. "What precisely does he need me to cooperate with?"

Edward pushed back his Stetson, looking uncomfortable. "He needs you to hold off getting married until he can gather enough evidence to make an arrest."

She caught her lower lip between her teeth. "In my experience, building a case against someone can take months, sometimes even years."

Every part of Pecos rebelled at the thought of waiting that long. Why, he'd marry her tonight — right now if a man of the cloth was present! He reached for her hand and threaded his fingers reassuringly through hers. As the Lord was his witness, they would find a way to be together as man and wife soon.

"There are never any guarantees, of course. The situation will play itself out however it's going to play itself out. However, I am confident the case will not take much longer," Edward hastened to assure. "It can't. We have every reason to believe Redwood is about to close the doors of his agency and skip town."

"Why?" Pecos scowled over at him, still not appreciating the high-handed way Edward had invaded the intimacy of his reunion with Meg.

"Because he never stays anywhere for long." Edward rubbed his hands together and held them out to the fire again. "His story about leaving a well-established business with his brother is a pile of horse dung. He has no brother. No family at all that the marshal can find. Clink Redwood was orphaned as a child, raised by a group of con artists, and eventually got sucked into their schemes. The rest of his cronies are either dead or in jail. He alone continues to travel from town to town, hoodwinking hopeful grooms into setting up those over-priced payment plans of his. He stays just long enough to bleed the fellas dry; then he moves on and starts all over again in the next town."

"If that's the case, how did you and Lacey ever get married?" Meg cried. "And what about Jesse and Iris?"

Pecos squeezed her hand again. He had the same questions.

Edward shrugged. "According to the marshal, Redwood usually marries off one or two couples fairly quickly to appear legitimate. Then he acquires a real looker as bait and starts his shenanigans."

"So he never actually intended to marry me off, eh?" Meg's lush mouth turned downward. "I was never more than a pretty face to him." She looked supremely disheartened over the discovery.

Pecos longed to assure her that she was so much more than a pretty face, but he held his tongue. He'd rather have a little privacy first before sharing all that was on his heart with her.

Edward grimaced. "No, marrying you off probably wasn't in his plans. Not that you'd ever have any trouble attracting a whole slew of suitors on your own. On top of being lovely, you are kindhearted, talented, and hardworking." He cast an admiring sideways glance at her. "It was diabolically clever of him to get you hired on at the inn. While Lacey and I were busy thanking the good Lord for our recent uptick in visitors, Redwood was benefiting from all the free advertisement for his services. Oh, and he got out of paying for your room and board, as well."

"Here and I thought I was the one being clever," Meg sighed. "Skating out of my last town on the coattails of a mail-order bride contract. Thanks to Clink Redwood and his schemes, all I did was leap out of the frying pan into the fire."

"Is that so?" Pecos decided it was finally time to distract her from her melancholy. He raised her hand to his mouth to kiss her chilly knuckles. "Methinks you accomplished quite a lot more than that. For one thing, you caught my heart and reeled it in."

"Pecos!" She gave a breathy chuckle. "You are not a fish."

He leaned closer to whisper for her ears alone, "In your hands, I am as helpless as one."

He was rewarded with another blush.

A clattering at the edge of the clearing had all their heads spinning around to observe the latest newcomer to their circle.

Jesse Hawling stomped closer to the fire, glaring ferociously at Pecos. He pointed at Edward. "What in the blazes is he doing here?"

With a hoot of joy, Edward stood. "It's good to see you again, deputy." He jogged forward, holding out a hand. "I hear congratulations are in order."

Jesse scowled at his outstretched hand. "For what?"

"Well, let's see," Edward teased. "Last time we parted ways, you were nothing more than a hard-nosed deputy, hell-bent on avenging the many wrongs that had been done to your family. And now you're a father." When Jesse still didn't shake his hand, he closed the distance between them to clap him on the back. Then he dropped his arms. "How in tarnation does that make us enemies again?"

"It doesn't." Jesse rubbed a hand over his beard, eyeing Edward through narrowed lids. "A missing house deed, however, might." His lips flattened. "Especially since you are one of the few souls in the world who knew its location."

Edward's expression didn't change. He merely reached inside his jacket.

Jesse whipped out a pair of pistols, training them on the innkeeper as he took a few steps back. "If I were you, I'd think very carefully about your next move, Remington."

"Believe me, I have." Edward's voice was cool and clipped as he removed a folded slip of paper from the inside pocket of his jacket. It glowed white in the moonlight. "You're going to want to look at this." He held it out between two fingers.

Jesse danced closer to snatch it from him. Unfolding it, he stared at it in shock. "This is the missing deed. How did you get it?" he demanded.

"From a pair of thieves." Edward pointed at the document. "They came to the inn, posing as painters. Being a suspicious man by nature, I searched their bags after I put them to work on the back veranda. Imagine my surprise when I discovered the deed to your farm tucked inside. You haven't, by any chance, had a room painted lately?"

"Of all the——!" Muttering something beneath his breath, Jesse stuffed the document inside the pocket of his fringed coat.

"May we start over?" Edward inquired quietly. He warily spread his arms. "It's been an awfully long time, my friend."

"I reckon it has been." Jesse clenched his jaw and enveloped the innkeeper in a somewhat sheepish hug.

CHAPTER 7: COURTING DISASTER

MEG

For the next several weeks, bounty hunters continued to traipse in and out of Christmas Mountain, making it unsafe for Meg to return to the inn. Instead of bemoaning the restrictions to her freedom, she made a point of enjoying the peace and beauty of Pecos' mountain home. It was, quite literally, built into the mountainside. One could have passed within a few feet of its entrance and been none the wiser about its existence.

Her guest chamber turned out to be a spacious cavern room. Though it was black as pitch, requiring a lantern to remain lit while she was indoors, it was warm and unexpectedly cozy. The Comanches had erected a stacked stone fireplace against one wall and piped the smoke out through an earthen chimney.

Her bed was a roughly hewn platform of split logs. However, so many animal furs were piled on top of it that it was nearly as soft as a down mattress. The walls of the cavern were lined with a collection of hand-painted tapestries, all of them depicting the beautiful Mustangs that the Comanches trained and rode. Two were of the majestic creatures in a full run across a set of ruby red mesas. Three others were close-ups of individual horses — a dappled red and white that resembled Paint, a black stallion rearing back on its hind legs, and a mare nuzzling her foal. The final tapestry depicted a lone rider with his heels dug into the horse's flanks as he raced through a mountain pass.

He was facing away from the painting, and his long, black hair flowed behind him in the wind. However, his feathered headdress and the gold bands around his biceps indicated he was someone of importance. A tribal chief, more than likely. The next time Meg saw Pecos, she would ask him if the man in the painting was him.

He'd promised to take her on a trail ride, since her ankle was so tremendously improved. The past few days she'd even been able to take a few tentative steps on it without wincing in pain. However, he was insisting that she wear a special boot he'd crafted for her, to shield the bone until it fully healed.

As she donned her tunic and leggings and tugged on his latest gift, a thick, bear fur coat, she rejoiced in the fact that she would finally be able to leave her crutch behind. She banked the fire in the hearth and glanced around her guest chamber one last time to ensure she wasn't leaving anything undone.

It was spotless. Her bed was made, and her toiletries were neatly stowed inside her travel bag. All she needed to do was turn off the lantern. However, she lingered an extra few seconds, unable to shake the feeling that her peaceful escape into the mountains was about to come to an end.

Either that, or I'm fretting over nothing. Though the town continued to experience a constant flow of visiting bounty hunters, most of them didn't stay for long. Fortunately, they thought they were searching for a man. It helped that Mav Peterson gossiped up a storm with each newcomer to the

General Store, sending them right back out of town on one wild goose chase after another.

Meg knew she wouldn't be able to stay holed up in the mountains forever, though. She was overdue for one of her quick showings in town, and she wasn't looking forward to it. It was her way of helping the undercover marshal keep up appearances with Clink Redwood.

It wasn't just the risk of encountering a bounty hunter that made her dread her trips into town, though. The latest rumors flying around about her were making her cringe. It was being said behind her back that she was something of a tease, lavishing her affections on any fellow who smiled in her direction. *Oh, gag me!* She couldn't wait to put an end to all the speculation by marrying Pecos. Most unfortunately, her dubious reputation had caused a resurgence in business at the mail-order bride agency. According to Thatcher Mills, Clink was raking in the money, hand over fist — money that Thatcher promised to return to its rightful owners once the case was closed.

With a resolute sigh, Meg bent over the lantern resting on the log nightstand next to her bed. She doused its flame. Then she marched straight for the tapestry covering the doorway leading from her chamber. A community fire was roaring in the main cavern on the other side.

Night Flyer was hovering near the shoulder of one of the older fellows, a man by the name of Dakota. His white hair was falling half over his face as he stirred something in his stew pot. He was the closest thing they had to a cook. Since she missed her job at Christmas Mountain Inn so much, she'd fallen into the habit of shadowing him to learn as much as possible about the cuisine of the Comanches.

Meg glided in their direction, sniffing the air. "It smells wonderful," she sang out. "What is on the menu today?"

Dakota glanced up at her approach, and his silvery eyes softened.

"Rattlesnake bites," Night Flyer supplied before his elder could say anything. "They're tough, stringy, and full of bones; but they're not too hard to choke down if you add a little salt."

She reached over to tweak one of his braids as she passed him. "No doubt I'll have an easier time swallowing whatever Dakota is simmering in his pot than half of your tall tales, including this one."

"Wild turkey," Dakota corrected with a knowing twinkle. His buckskin leggings were streaked with stains from cooking, since he generally wiped his hands on his clothing. "Beans, onions, ham." His English was broken, but he knew how to get right to the point by reciting the main ingredients.

"It sounds delicious," she assured. "I hope Pecos and I are back in time for lunch."

"We will not be." Pecos' husky baritone carried across the cavern.

She flushed as she glanced his way, drinking in his broad shoulders and bronze features that had become so dear to her. He wasn't the handsomest man she'd ever encountered, with his hard, angular features, but he was by far the most arresting. There was something about his brooding gaze that made her heartbeat accelerate every time their gazes met. He was her trail guide and self-appointed protector, her closest friend, and the man she would soon marry. Not soon enough, though. Thatcher Mills' investigation was dragging on much longer than either of them had hoped.

"Good morning, Chief," she teased, sashaying toward him in her fluffy fur coat.

His coal colored eyes raked her from head to foot. "What happened to your crutch?"

"I threw it off the nearest cliff," she lied, tilting her head sassily at him.

His gaze glinted with humor. "In that case, I will have to carry you to your horse." He swooped closer to scoop her up in his arms.

She giggled and slid her arms around his neck. "Are you going to continue growling at me like a bear after we are wed?"

"Yes." He feigned a low, menacing rumble that sounded more like a rabid wolf than a bear as he nuzzled her cheek.

"Forget the rattlesnake bites," Night Flyer muttered from behind them. "I'll just climb inside the stewpot myself. How else is an innocent lad supposed to un-see and un-hear so much sappiness?"

"Aw!" Meg allowed her voice to carry across the room. "I think he's trying to tell us to do our kissing outside."

"Too bad." Pecos' tone was unsympathetic as he continued to nuzzle his way along the line of her chin. "He's about to be a grown man. He could use a bit of education on certain topics."

Night Flyer fell into a fit of gagging noises, loud ones that had Meg dissolving into laughter as Pecos carried her outside.

"Oh-h-h-h!" she breathed, gazing around them. "Oh, Pecos! It's so beautiful."

"Yes, it is." His arms tightened around her, and she could feel his smoldering gaze on her face.

The first snow of the season was falling, not fast and heavy, though. Big, fat, fluffy flakes fluttered down on their noses and cheeks. The mountains were breathtaking all year long, but they were especially gorgeous today with their fresh white caps.

"Kiss me, Two Dark Moons," Pecos commanded huskily.

She turned her face to his, and his mouth found hers. The warmth of his ardor melted the snowflakes on her lips. She could sense the leashed energy radiating from him and taste his impatience.

"I want you for my wife," he growled between kisses. "I am tired of waiting."

"I'm tired of waiting, too." She fisted a hand in his silky hair, giving it a light tug to bring his mouth closer still.

He was the first to break off their kiss. "I will find a way for us to wed soon," he promised hoarsely, "if I have to hog-tie that rapscallion matchmaker myself and force a confession from him." He strode with her across the clearing to the nearest grazing Mustang. It was Paint, the speckled horse he normally rode. However, any time they went out on the trails together, he insisted she be the one to ride Paint.

"I don't mind riding one of the other Mustangs," she protested as he set her atop Paint. "I know this one is your favorite." She was secretly proud of how quickly she'd learned to ride bareback. It was so different from riding in a saddle. It made her feel more connected to the horse, somehow, like they were one creature instead of two.

"I like them all," Pecos assured, "but he is the best trained. The only reason I've been riding him so often lately is to hone his skills for you."

"Oh." She was touched by his thoughtfulness. "That's so kind of you."

"It's necessary." He leaped astride Midnight, the other horse she'd noticed him riding fairly often. "I didn't want these wildlings mercilessly jostling your injury."

"I am so happy to be rid of my crutch," she confessed. "My ankle truly feels as good as new." She hoped she never had a reason to hop around on a crutch again.

"Not quite as good as new yet," he cautioned. "It is still healing on the inside. You must be patient. It would be all too easy to re-injure it right now if you overdo it."

"Then I shall be extra careful." She made a face at him. "Where are you taking me?"

"To town." His jaw tightened.

Disappointment coursed through her. "Like this?" She glanced down in dismay at her thick fur coat and leather leggings. Dressed as she was, any onlooker couldn't even be sure if she were female.

"Well, not quite all the way to town. To Christmas Mountain Inn," he amended. "Lacey has been begging me to bring you for a visit, claiming Malachi is in desperate need of an aunt's influence."

"That he is." Meg chuckled. It was a made-up excuse if she'd ever heard one, but she was delighted that Pecos found it compelling enough to act on.

"She also has the church pastor coming over this morning for Malachi's baby dedication," he continued, "and she wanted us to be there for it."

"Oh, how wonderful!" Meg raised sparkling eyes to his. She hadn't been able to attend church since the bounty hunters arrived in town, so it would be wonderful to attend any service at all, even a baby dedication. It was sweet of Lacey to include her and Pecos in such a special occasion.

Pecos gave her an inscrutable look. He followed it with a sharp whistle that made both horses leap into motion.

"It's like you speak their language," Meg sighed, amazed at how responsive the creatures were to his every whistle, word, and movement. He knew the language of the Mustangs.

"I've worked with horses since I was old enough to toddle my first step." He wasn't bragging; he was simply stating a fact.

"If you don't mind me asking, where did you toddle that first step?" she asked suddenly. "I've never asked where you were from."

"My Pa is from a reservation in Colorado," he supplied

in a tight voice that told her it wasn't a pleasant experience. "He escaped as a teen, stowed away on a train, and ended up in Texas. Even though a lot of folks weren't hiring Native Americans at the time, he managed to find a job as a seasonal worker on Carlson Ranch. You might have heard of it. It used to be the biggest cattle ranch in the area."

She shook her head. "I am too new to town. I don't know many people yet."

"He met Ma there. She was the daughter of the rancher who hired him. A fine, upstanding Christian man who lost no sleep over my ma courting a fellow whose skin was a different color than hers. What he did have a problem with was the fact that my pa had never darkened the doorsteps of a church before. That soon changed."

A twinkle lit Pecos' dark gaze. "Initially, the only place he allowed my pa to escort my ma was to church. She sang in the choir, so he got to walk her to her practices as well as the Sunday services. Eventually, Mr. Carlson let pa come sit with her on the porch swing at the farmhouse, but that was only after pa gave his life to the Lord."

"He was old school," Meg murmured. She found his story to be both amusing and heartwarming. It made her wish she'd gotten to meet Mr. Carlson. He sounded like a generous, kindhearted man.

"My grandfather was a good man. Alas, the town wasn't all that accepting of a mixed marriage. Nor were they very accepting of his half-breed grandson. He was more or less blackballed by the other citizens, which made it difficult to keep his horse breeding business going. He ended up selling his ranch at a steep discount and moving to the edge of town to live out his days on a few hundred acres of mountain property."

"The property you now own." Though Meg appreciated

knowing more about the man she was going to marry, it was a bittersweet story.

"Yes, and the property I plan to keep, Lord willing." He looked and sounded determined. "I recently spoke to Edward Remington about a business proposition."

"Tell me about it." She blinked away the latest snowflakes that had fallen on her lashes.

"I am going to build horse stables, a few training rings, and a racing track, so I can start hosting rodeos for the townsfolk."

"Pecos!" She was astounded by the enormity of such an undertaking.

"Me and my fellow Comanches will do as much of the work as we can and hire out only what we have to."

She blinked in astonishment. "Will it be expensive to build?" Where would he get that kind of money?

He turned his head to squarely meet her gaze. "It will, but I have some money saved from my Mustang business. The Lord has blessed us with steadily rising profits."

Her lips parted in surprise. So she was marrying a wealthy man. Or at least a well-heeled one...

"Edward also advised me to build you a house, Two Dark Moons. A two-story with all the trimmings right down to a pair of rockers on the front porch. He said it would help convince the townsfolk that I am civilized."

"Pecos," she breathed, stricken at the realization that he was still facing the same ridicule his father and grandfather had faced. "I love your canyon home. It's so beautiful with the way it's built right into the mountain, and it's safe. Safer than I've ever felt before."

"Thank you. Knowing that you've been happy living with my people makes me happy. But Edward is right. Times are changing. I must change, too."

"Don't change too much," she pleaded softly. "I love you

just the way you are."

His dark head swung abruptly in her direction, making her realize what she'd said. *I love you just the way you are.* She blushed at her display of boldness, but it was true. She did love him, wholly and hopelessly.

He didn't say a word as they passed over his property line to the rear grounds of the Christmas Mountain Inn. As they rode around to the front, they found three other horses tethered to the hitching post. There was also a team of horses hitched to a covered wagon.

"It looks as if they've invited half the town." Meg's heart thumped with apprehension since she'd been avoiding most people for the past few weeks.

"One of them is Thatcher Mills," Pecos noted, leaping from Midnight's back. He produced a rope to tether him to the far end of the post. Then he assisted Meg to the ground.

She wrinkled her nose at him as they worked together to tether her horse. "How can you be so sure?"

"I recognized his saddle bag. He also keeps renting the same horse from the livery."

She was suddenly no longer excited about attending the baby dedication ceremony. Sure, she adored little Malachi. However, if the undercover marshal was waiting for her inside the inn, he would expect her to keep up appearances and pretend to be courting him...again. It was a charade she was deathly tired of.

Wishing like mad that she and Pecos had simply gone for a gallop in the snow, she murmured, "Let's get this over with, shall we?" She took unholy delight in the fact that she was wearing the buckskin tunic and leggings Pecos had gifted her, along with her toasty warm bear fur coat. She was done with "keeping up appearances." Her clothing would scream louder than words that she belonged to someone else besides the marshal.

"If you wish." Pecos blocked her path to the porch stairs with his large frame. "When we return home, we should talk to Sanko about reserving a date with his minister friend to marry us. It is time."

"It is?" she gasped.

"If you're willing. I wasn't waiting to please the marshal. I wanted the time to properly court you. If you truly love me, then I have already accomplished everything I set out to do."

"Oh, Pecos!" she exclaimed.

"We must hurry inside now." He reached out to flick a snowflake from her cheek. "If I stop to kiss you again, we will never make it to the baby dedication."

As usual, however, he was more concerned about her well-being than "appearances." He didn't hesitate to snake an arm around her waist and all but lifted her up the frosty porch stairs. The veranda had been recently swept clear of snow. However, more continued to drift down, coating the rocking chairs and floor with a fresh layer of whiteness.

Meg raised her gloved hand to knock on the front door of the inn, but it unexpectedly flew open.

Lacey's distressed features appeared. Her red-gold curls were askew, and her eyes were red-rimmed from weeping. "Come in," she choked, taking a step back.

"Lacey!" Knowing something was terribly wrong, Meg quickly stepped over the threshold and reached for her friend's shoulders. "Are you well?" The homey rag rugs and gingham curtains, along with the scent of baking bread, made her realize just how much she'd missed working at the place.

"No!" the innkeeper's wife sobbed. "Please believe me when I say I had no idea this is what they intended for you. Otherwise I would have never asked you to come."

Meg stiffened at the sound of a pair of pistols being cocked.

"Meg Chastain," Thatcher Mills' gravelly voice droned,

"you are under arrest for the robbery of Midtown Bank in Riverville."

She met his icy blue gaze, utterly shocked by his betrayal. She'd confided in him all there was to know about her past and everything she'd been running from, and he'd claimed he believed her innocence.

Pecos' hand tightened on her shoulder.

"Step back!" the man at his side ordered harshly. He was a stocky fellow with longish auburn hair. One unruly lock was dangling across his left eye. Even more notable was the silver badge glinting from his shirt.

"Sheriff Dawson!" Lacey gasped. "Is this truly necessary?"

"Unfortunately, ma'am." He eyed Pecos dispassionately. "I can well imagine your thoughts on the matter, sir, but do not make this any harder than it has to be. If you put up a fight, you'll be arrested alongside Miss Chastain. We need for you to step away and let the law do its job. I assure you justice will prevail."

The sheriff's words made Meg's knees shake. She and Pecos were sorely outnumbered; there was no point in fighting or trying to run. "He's right, Pecos." Her voice hitched over a lump of emotion as she added, "Please. Just do as he says." There was no need for both of them to end up behind bars.

Her words were met by stony silence. However, his hand lifted from her shoulder. She immediately missed the weight of it and the warmth.

"Do something, sweetheart!" Lacey sobbed from the other side of the foyer.

Meg had no idea who she was speaking to until Edward appeared, white-faced, and approached the marshal. "Miss Chastain is my client. I'll be accompanying her to the station."

"This is preposterous! I've never taken a penny from

anyone in my life, Edward!" She shuddered as she faced him. "I am innocent, and everyone here knows it." *Say something. Please!*

"We will discuss the case in private," he assured in what was probably supposed to be a soothing voice, but she was beyond soothing.

She returned her attention to the marshal, asking in frenzied disbelief, "Why are you doing this?" She read weary resignation in his features and wondered what had changed his mind. His hat was missing, revealing short-clipped hair so blonde it was nearly white, and his shoulders were bunched with tension. He gave her a slight head shake, as if warning her not to say too much.

"Because robbing a bank is a heinous crime," an all-too familiar voice mocked.

"Jones?" she gasped. Jones Storm was in the room, too? Her ex-partner and the source of all the false accusations. Oh, this was bitter! This was cruel! "What are you doing here, Jones?" She blinked back the hotness of tears as she lifted her chin to meet his scrutiny.

"Making sure you don't get away with your crimes, that's what." He towered over her, using every inch of his impressive height in the attempt to make her feel small and helpless. He'd done it a thousand times in the past, usually in a teasing manner.

The only emotions riding his handsome ebony features now were fury and abject bitterness. She was momentarily stunned. She'd never seen so much venom in him before.

She shook her head at him, utterly perplexed. "Why would you make such a claim?" she begged. They'd been partners, for crying out loud! Like family! "Just tell me why!"

"Oh, do not bother playing the part of the innocent," he snarled. "There is no one else who knew my comings and goings like you did, no one else who could've so thoroughly framed me for a crime I did not commit and make it look so convincing." He was dressed in solid black, from his Stetson to his patched overcoat to his dusty boots.

"What are you talking about?" she cried piteously.

"Not another word, Meg. I mean it," Edward commanded. He smoothed his white collar and gave the lapels of his black suit jacket a yank to straighten it. "We will get to the bottom of this at the station. Until then, I'm asking you to bite your tongue and trust me."

Trust you? Once upon a time, Meg had trusted Jones Storm with all of her heart — he'd been like a brother to her — and look at where such a foolish sentiment had gotten her.

"I want to be informed of her bail as soon as it is set," Pecos announced harshly. "Whatever the amount, I will pay it."

"No, please." Tears of anguish dripped down her cheeks. "It'll bankrupt you." She did not wish for Pecos to go broke bailing her out of jail. He had a rodeo business to start up, construction to commence, and a lot of Comanche comrades depending on him for their next meal.

"She's right. Do you remember the matter we discussed, my friend?" Edward asked cryptically. "You may need to rethink your position on it and do as I advised. It's the only way you're going to be able to raise that kind of money."

"I am so sorry." Meg sniffed damply, willing Pecos to understand. "I did not mean to drag you into my troubles like this."

"I am not sorry, Two Dark Moons." His voice was cold and utterly devoid of emotion. "The good Lord will help us find a way out. He always does."

Jones Storm threw his dark hands in the air. "Am I the only one hearing this? Clearly, they are discussing Miss Chastain's stash of loot. If this doesn't prove her guilt to you, I don't know what will!"

CHAPTER 8: GOOD, OLD FASHIONED DETECTIVE WORK

MEG

"The truth, Mr. Storm. The truth is what will prove her innocence or her guilt." Sheriff Rick Dawson resolutely faced Jones Storm. He lowered his weapon, but he did not place it back in his holster. "You'll be needing to come with us to the station as well, to file an official statement."

Jones eyed the Sheriff's weapon that was still at the ready. "Why, certainly, Sheriff." The earlier venom in his voice was replaced with a mountain of sarcasm. "I reckon I look like the real villain here, eh?" He held up his hands, palms facing inward. "What, with skin as black as sin?"

"Don't!" Meg quavered to Jones. He'd always worn a chip on his shoulder the size of Texas. She hated the thought of him ending up in a jail cell next to hers, solely because of his insolence. "Don't do this, please. In case you haven't noticed, we're in enough trouble as it is."

His inky black brows shot upward at her sisterly scolding. It took him a moment to recover his indignant aplomb. "Speak for yourself." He hunched his shoulders in disgust and pivoted away from her. "You're a wanted criminal on the run.

They're only taking me in for questioning because I am black."

His righteous indignation was what ultimately convinced her that he was, indeed, innocent. "Oh, Jones," she murmured tearfully, so relieved that she wanted to run and throw her arms around him and beg his forgiveness. *I was so wrong to suspect you, so wrong to leave town without an explanation, without begging for your help, which you would have so freely given.* Jones Storm was no criminal. He was exactly the man she remembered him to be, right down to the short fuse on his abominable temper.

There was a momentary hesitation in his march to the front door. Then again, maybe she only imagined it. He stomped outside ahead of them, making the floorboards on the porch rattle and the horses whinny in alarm.

She stared after him in agony. His innocence threw every last one of her previous theories out the window. It had to mean someone else was trying to frame one or both of them for the bank robbery that neither of them had committed. It also followed that someone had purposely driven the current wedge between them. But who? Alas, no quick and easy answers were forthcoming.

The hardest thing about leaving Christmas Mountain Inn in handcuffs was having to walk past Pecos Carlson. In all the months Meg had known him, he'd maintained a stoic expression. Not so this morning. He was glaring so ferociously at the men leading her down the stairs of the veranda, that she was terrified the situation would end in bloodshed.

She could think of no words adequate to express her love for him, or her regrets over how she was leaving things between them. All she could do was silently beg him with her eyes to stand down. *Be wise and be safe. I love you!*

She could feel his scorching gaze on her as she was loaded into the back of the waiting wagon. Interestingly enough, the sheriff was the one who climbed into the driver's seat and took the reins, while the undercover marshal and Jones slid onto the bench across from her. The canvas covering of the wagon fell into place behind them, shielding them from those who were watching from the inn.

Right before the wagon started to roll, Edward Remington climbed aboard to join them. "Don't shoot," he pleaded as he took a seat next to Meg. "I am unarmed." He held up his hands. "Search me if you wish."

"That won't be necessary." Thatcher Mills turned to Jones Storm and arched his blonde brows suggestively. "Since you are so fond of grandstanding, you should say your piece first."

"Me? Grandstanding?" Jones placed his hands mockingly on his chest. "Why, I wouldn't think of it!"

Meg's head spun between the two men as it slowly dawned on her that they were jesting like old friends. Clearly, they were in cahoots. But what did it mean? For her? For her arrest? For the case itself?

Jones' upper lip curled sardonically as he met her gaze. "Tell me something, little sis. Why, on God's green earth, did you take off running the way you did?"

She blinked in astonishment at his rapid change of tone and demeanor.

"You do not need to answer that question, Meg," Edward interjected quickly. "In fact, I advise you not to."

"Oh, give way!" Jones snarled, glancing his way. "Of course I know she didn't rob that bank!" He returned his attention to Meg. "But the very idea that you assumed I did..." He shook his head, looking ferociously angry and equally hurt. "I know I have a bad temper, but you know that, as well. You know me better than anyone else — the good, the bad, and everything in between. At least I thought you did," he ended hoarsely.

Meg shot a quick glance at Edward, but he did not reiterate his urging to remain silent.

"I did," she assured damply. "I mean, I do. And you're right, Jones. I've known it for some time now. Running only made me look guilty," she sighed, "but I wasn't thinking clearly. The evidence against you was so compelling. Then that dratted WANTED poster surfaced with my face on it, and I panicked, thinking you were framing me for the robbery." She shook her head. "I, ah...it broke my heart. I reckon I ran because I truly thought I had no reason left to stay." She pressed a hand to her chest as she relived the sickening feeling of betrayal.

"You believe my innocence now, though." He held her gaze steadily. "Why?"

"Because I finally looked you in the eyes, I reckon." She waved a hand helplessly. "Because I'm looking you in the eyes right now, and all I can see is how wrong I was to doubt you." Tears stung the backs of her eyelids. "You're the closest thing I ever had to a family, Jones." Her voice broke. "I've missed you. So much!"

"Aww, shucks!" He pushed off the bench. Nudging Edward over, he plopped down beside her and gathered her in his arms, pressing her head beneath his chin. "I'm still mad at you, but I've missed you, too. Ain't nobody rushing to be my family since you left town." She was assailed by the familiar scent of his hand-mixed aftershave cream.

Her tears turned cold on her cheeks. "If you believe I'm innocent, too, then why are we on our way to the jailhouse?"

Jones abruptly let her go. "To protect you, of course!" He scowled down at her. "Some very bad hombres are closing in on you, sis. No way could I just stand by and let that happen." A smirk fought for supremacy over his scowl. "Plus, there's a mammoth bounty on the heads of the real desperadoes. I wouldn't mind getting a cut of that. No, sirre-e-e!" He gave a delighted whistle.

She gave a huff of indignation. "There's also a $2500 bounty on my head, in case you've forgotten."

"Mere pocket change in comparison." He waggled a finger at her, looking superior. "We're talking fifteen grand, sweetie. Mercy, but a fellow could retire on that kind of money!"

"Then why were you so dead set against pursuing them back when we were partners?" she demanded. "It's partly what convinced me you were in on the robbery."

He glanced away, looking shamefaced. "For a reason I couldn't bring myself to tell you at the time. I was afraid you'd never forgive me. I'm not certain I'll ever forgive myself for it."

"I'm your sister," she spluttered. "Or as good as. What could you possibly have done that's so unforgivable?"

He hung his head. "I made a terrible mistake," he confessed. "I met a feller at a diner before you left town. Real likable chap, though it was clear to me from the start that he'd only befriended me because of you."

"Me! Why?"

Jones rolled his eyes at the marshal. "Do you see the nonsense I have to put up with when she's around?"

"Sadly, yes." The amused look Thatcher Mills sent Meg was enough to make her blush. "She's viewed me like a bug needing to be squashed the entire time we've supposedly been courting."

She rounded on him indignantly. "I most certainly have not. I've played my part rather well, I think."

His blonde brows rose alarmingly. "I believe you're forgetting about your very public kiss with a certain tribal chief."

She nibbled her lower lip in agitation, hardly knowing what to say to that. *Fine. Maybe I haven't played my part so perfectly, after all.*

"Back to my story about that fellow at the diner." Jones made a rueful face. "He cottoned to you, and wanted me to make the introduction. In hindsight, I should've guessed who he was sooner than I did. All along, I thought he looked familiar, but I didn't connect the dots right away. I reckon I was too busy being horrified that he'd guessed you weren't a man, despite the hat and trousers you always wore on the job."

Meg was thoroughly perplexed by now. "Well, who was he?"

"John Younger, as it turns out."

She felt her eyes bug out. "John Younger, as in the James-Younger Gang?" An honest-to-gosh friend and fellow criminal of Jesse James, himself?

"Yes. That John." Jones rubbed his hands over his eyes, as if trying to erase the memory.

"Oh, my lands!" she breathed, finally understanding. The Younger brothers were the next fellows she and Jones had been hoping to chase down and collar for the bounty on their heads — the same bounty that Jones had so vehemently argued to her that they should forget about. "So that's why we argued, and that's why you wanted to forego that particular bounty."

"Yes." He spread his large hands. "John knew who we were, and I think he knew exactly when I guessed his identity in return. I didn't say anything to him about it, of course. I continued to call him by the fake name he'd introduced himself as, but his suspicions were tickled."

He shook his head in disgust. "He and his brothers robbed the Riverville Bank the following week, and suddenly your face was on the WANTED poster for it? Nah!" Jones swung his head from side to side. "That's way too much of a coincidence for me. After I recognized the chap, I became a loose end that needed tying up. You and me both."

"You should have told me." Meg was sad that he hadn't. They could've avoided all the misunderstandings that had torn them apart. She sought out the marshal's gaze for confirmation. "I reckon this means I am not really under arrest?"

He shook his head soberly. "No, but we'd like to offer you protective custody until the real outlaws are brought to justice."

She raised her chin. "Actually, Pecos was doing a really swell job of keeping me safe before you showed up."

Jones barked out a laugh. "If that's the demon-eyed fellow who nearly burnt a hole through my hat with his eyes..."

"He's the man I intend to marry, Jones."

"Ah. That explains a lot." He folded his arms, looking wry. "For a moment there at the inn, I thought he might pull a hatchet on me."

By the time they arrived at the sheriff's office, the snow was falling more thickly. An inch or so of whiteness covered the hard-packed dirt street.

Meg's brain was still buzzing with dozens of unanswered questions. "You're not going to set any bail, are you?" she mused quietly.

"No." Jones leaped off the back of the wagon and turned around to reach for her. "Thatch?" He waited until the undercover marshal hopped to the ground before he finished lowering Meg to her feet.

The sheriff and marshal had their weapons drawn and were scanning both ends of Main Street.

"Follow me," Sheriff Rick Dawson ordered quietly. He jogged across the weathered front porch of his office and threw open the front door. "I'd like to place the two of you in holding cells." He pointed between Meg and Jones. "I apologize in advance for the necessity. However, we need to be able to spread the word about your arrest and make it look like the bounty is about to be paid out."

"Which the Youngers never cared about in the first place," she pointed out. It made perfect sense now. They merely needed for her to be arrested and enough buzz about it to hit the news for them to figure out her location. Then they would come and finish the job.

☙❧

COME NIGHTFALL, MEG FOUND HERSELF ON A THIN COT inside a chilly jail cell. A gray-headed man was already asleep in the cell next to hers. Or pretending to sleep.

"Jones?" she muttered softly into the darkness.

"What is it, sis?" He rolled to his side on his narrow bed, facing her through the bars of the cell directly across from hers. There were four cells in all, though the one next to his was empty.

"I'm not overly thrilled about being in jail tonight, but I'm very glad you found me."

"I'm glad, too." He sounded sad. "I sure do hate the thought of losing you all over again when you wed that dark-eyed demon, though."

"Jones!" A chuckle escaped her, louder than she intended. She quickly clapped a hand over her mouth, glancing at the sleeping man beside her. "He's a good man. A very, very good man!"

"He'd better be," Jones snarled. He seemed utterly unconcerned about keeping his volume down. "Or he'll be answering to your big brother, now that I'm in town."

"I can't wait to introduce you," she returned happily.

"No need. We already met," he reminded, pulling his blankets up to his chin.

"That wasn't a real introduction," she scoffed. "Everyone was growling at each other, and he was having visions of skinning you alive, I'm sure."

Jones pretended to shudder. "Now *that's* a lovely thought to go to sleep on!"

"Indeed," the gentleman in the cell next to hers drawled. "I, for one, would love to get some sleep over here."

"Oh, gracious!" Meg lowered her voice to barely above a whisper. "We're so sorry for disturbing you."

"I was only jesting." The man sat up on his cot, looking so awake that she discerned he hadn't been sleeping at all, but rather eavesdropping on them. "This is the most excitement I've had in weeks. No, months." He scratched a hand through his overgrown board. "Nah, it's probably been years, come to think of it."

"Years!" Meg exclaimed. Her sympathies were tugged by his jovial tone, wondering how anyone could sound so nonchalant about being in jail for that long. Why hadn't the sheriff mentioned they'd be having a cell mate? A hardened criminal, no less!

"Aye, years, but it's hardly an interesting story. I'd much rather hear yours first." He pulled up his knees in front of him and slung his arms around them. Then he fixed his rapt expression on her. "Starting with how you caught the eye of a certain Comanche chief in town."

She caught her breath. "How did you—?"

"It was the markings on your tunic." He winked at her. "I grew up in this part of the country, so I'd recognize the work of Chief Pecos and his tribe from a mile away."

"Ah." She blinked, not quite ready to discuss her and Pecos' relationship with a perfect stranger. "I don't believe we ever got around to introducing ourselves. I'm Meg Chastain, a mail-order bride. Well," she corrected, rolling her eyes, "I was supposed to be. That, too, is a long story. One I don't have the energy to go into tonight."

"You see there?" The older gentleman spread his hands. "I knew your story would be more interesting than mine."

She smiled and peered a little closer at him. His features seemed strangely familiar, though she was certain they'd never met.

"I'm Jones Storm, old man. Her brother." Jones gripped the bars of his cell and brought his face flush with the iron. "So you'd best keep your eyes, hands, and thoughts to yourself. You hear?"

The fellow gave a cackle of mirth. "You don't look much like her, if you don't mind me pointing it out."

"As a matter of fact, I do mind." Jones hitched one shoulder to angle his body toward Meg, essentially edging the man out of their conversation.

"Oh, Jones!" she scolded. "At least let him introduce himself. What harm could there be in that?"

"I could go on for hours," Jones informed her flatly, "but that would take far longer than the topic is worth." Glaring across the small prison block at their neighbor, he commanded, "Go on, then. State your name and be done with it."

There was a moment of silence. "Hawling." The man's merry manner evaporated, and something much darker and colder slid into its place. "The name is Hawling."

Meg's forehead wrinkled. "Hawling! You aren't, by any chance, related to Jesse, Jack, and Jonah, are you?"

"I am their father." Mr. Hawling's shoulders sagged.

"Oh, my!" she murmured. Her mind was flooded with questions, but she hardly knew where to begin. "I, ah..."

"I'm tired," the man announced abruptly. "Perhaps, we can chew the fat again in the morning." He rolled to his side and turned his back to her. "Feel free to talk all you please. It truly will not disturb me. Good night."

Meg stared at him, open-mouthed.

Jones finally cleared his throat. "I believe we were discussing how I'm about to lose you to your fire-breathing dragon of a groom. He seriously scalded my backside with a single look." For emphasis, Jones reached around to rub said body part as if it still stung.

She snickered. "You're a nut. And you won't be losing me to anyone. The day we're wed, you'll be gaining a brother."

"Brother-in-law," he corrected sourly.

"Same thing."

"Not even." He huffed. "That blasted Native—"

"Pecos," she interrupted. "He has a name, and it's Pecos Carlson."

"You're marrying a man named after a bloody river?"

She chuckled again. "Yes. Doesn't it have the most romantic ring to it?" She closed her eyes so she could remember Pecos' beautiful dark eyes gazing into hers.

"Ugh!" Jones rolled to his side with a huff. "Pray assure me you are not kissing him inside your head over there."

"And if I am?" she teased, blushing into the darkness.

"Then I'll be kissing you back," a low baritone voice answered.

Meg gave a surprised yip of recognition and jumped to her feet as Pecos emerged from the shadows. She blushed harder, wondering how much of her conversation with Jones he'd overheard. But it hardly mattered. He was here, and she couldn't have been more glad to see him.

"How did you talk them into letting you visit me?" She clasped the bars between them with both hands.

He placed his hands over hers. "Persistence. Be assured I wore them down to a nubbin on the topic."

She drank in his handsome bronze features in the moonlight. She should have known he wouldn't let even a jail cell keep them apart. Though their circumstances were less than ideal, she decided to take advantage of the opportunity and introduce the two men she adored most in the world. "Pecos,

I'd like you to meet my brother, Jones Storm. Jones, this is Pecos Carlson, my affianced."

"Pleased to meet you." Jones faked a yawn, though his stretch was real. "Now if you'll just mosey on out of here so we can get some sleep."

"But he just got here!" The white light pouring through the tiny square window above them surrounded Pecos like a silver halo. Though Jones had jokingly referred to him as a demon, Meg thought he looked more like a dark angel of mercy.

"I have a better idea." Pecos leaned against the bars, pressing his face to them. "You go on to sleep, while your sister and I—"

Meg stood on her tiptoes to press her mouth to his, silencing him.

His lips moved hungrily over hers — seeking, cherishing, and possessing.

Jones made a gagging sound and tossed his pillow across his narrow cell. It slammed into the bars in a muted thud of fabric. "I'm still here, remember?"

Pecos took his time kissing her. Then he slowly raised his head. "Did you hear something?" he inquired in a falsely innocent voice. "It was either the screech of a bird or the squawk of a rusty hinge."

"Very funny," Jones growled. "That's why everybody here is laughing. Oh, wait. We're not."

"Good," Pecos said evenly, "because the fact that I intend to marry your sister is no laughing matter." His fingers tightened over hers.

"I don't recall giving you my permission." Jones' voice was testy.

"And I don't recall asking for it." Pecos leaned in again to lightly nip at Meg's lips. "But it will make her very happy if you give it, anyway."

"Says who?" her brother demanded.

"Says me," she sighed against Pecos' mouth.

"Egad!" Jones exclaimed. "Are you two kissing again?"

❧

IN THE END, MEG THREW HER BEDROLL ON THE FLOOR next to the bars. Pecos stretched his legs out on the other side of them and tipped back his head against the wall. They held hands through the bars and eventually went to sleep. He didn't take his leave of her until the wee hours of the morning.

"I'll be back, Two Dark Moons," he promised. He squeezed her fingers one last time. Then he disappeared into the darkness.

By the time Jones awoke, the sheriff was bursting through the door with the news that another bank robbery had occurred in the middle of the night. Both Meg and Jones had been confined behind bars while it happened. Thus, the timing of the robbery proved their innocence all over again.

However, since the bank robbery meant that the real robbers were nearby, the marshal and sheriff decided it was too good of an opportunity to pass up. They spent all day spreading the word about the double arrest of Jones and Meg, figuring the Youngers wouldn't be able to resist the opportunity to take a stab at tying up two loose ends at once.

"Easiest money I ever did earn," Jones bragged from his cell mid-morning. "We shoulda thought of this a long time ago — using ourselves as bait and earning money while we eat and sleep."

"So that's what's really going on here, eh?" Mr. Hawling abruptly rose from his cot and moved to the bars of his cell, gripping them in both hands. "You're innocent." The wistfulness in his tone was unmistakable.

"Eh..." Meg shrugged uncomfortably, wishing Jones had kept his mouth shut. "Innocent of some things. Guilty of others. You know how it is." She paced the narrow cell — four steps in one direction, quick pivot, then four steps in the other direction.

"I do." His smile was sad. "I knew the two of you were different the moment you walked in. I've had my share of thugs for cell mates, and you most definitely do not fit the bill."

"Neither do you," Jones announced from the other side of the room. "My sister and I have dealt with a decent number of thugs, as well. You are not one of them."

"Thank you."

Meg hoped Jesse's father would say more, but he lapsed into a brand of silence that did not brook more questions.

Jones sipped noisily on a mug of coffee that one of the clerks had delivered. His long legs were propped on his cot, lending him the leisure air of a prince in a palace.

"Ol' Sheriff Dawson has agreed to split the Youngers' bounties between the two of us when we catch them like rats in a trap." He sent her a sly wink. "Be assured I negotiated the fine details of our agreement before assisting in your fake arrest."

"You're all heart," she snapped, wishing she had something to throw at him. *Lord, help me. I could use a whole pot of that coffee this morning, maybe two pots.*

"You're welcome," Jones retorted cheerfully.

CHAPTER 9: TURNING POINT
PECOS

Alas, none of Jones' dream about making money while he slept came to fruition. Word reached them three days later that the Younger brothers had perished in a shoot-out in Missouri. It meant there would be no bounty money split between Jones and Meg.

Both Thatcher Mills and Sheriff Dawson accompanied Pecos into the holding cell to release their newest "prisoners."

"Please tell me this is all a bad dream," Jones groaned. His princely demeanor was gone. He mainly looked hungry. "I needed that money." He curled his large body off the cot and stood to stretch, giving a loud yawn.

Pecos couldn't help noticing how baggy his shirt and trousers hung on his too-thin frame before he yanked his tattered overcoat over them. The black fabric was thread-bare in several spots, making Pecos wonder how the fellow expected to stay warm during this winter weather.

The sheriff unlocked Meg's cell first. "Pray forgive the sparse accommodations of my jailhouse, madam." He ushered her from the cell with a gallant flourish that nearly unseated his Stetson from his auburn waves. "No doubt you're accustomed to the comforts at Christmas Mountain Inn."

"Nonetheless, I appreciate your hospitality." Despite the buckskin leggings she wore, she bent her knees in a faux curtsey. "In my previous line of work, your jail would qualify as one of our more upscale stopovers. More often than not, we threw our bedrolls under the stars."

It was a stark reminder to Pecos that the woman he was about to marry had been raised in much humbler circumstances than the live-off-the-land existence he'd chosen for himself. It made his upcoming plans to acclimate more to the white man's world not seem as bitter as they'd originally tasted. The fact that he was going to be building a home for Two Dark Moons was, well, something he was suddenly and tremendously looking forward to.

"Sleeping under the stars isn't so bad," Jones exclaimed, waving his hands dramatically toward the heavens. "They're God's own nightlights. I look forward to doing so again."

Meg stepped closer to Pecos. "That's his way of saying he has no place to go," she hissed.

He longed to take her in his arms and longed to sample another one of her sweet kisses. However, the twitchiness of her stance told him she was anxious to be gone from the stone walls of the prison.

Holding her lovely, dark gaze, Pecos announced, "Mr. Storm, I could sorely use another set of hands for an ongoing project."

"Is that so?" Jones struck a bored pose, pretending to cover a yawn.

But Pecos could hear the interest in his voice. And the hunger. "I'm in the middle of constructing a rodeo facility. Boarding stables, performance rings, and a race track. Seeing as how you're about to become family..."

"Oh, I see where this is going!" Jones stepped out of his

cell the moment the sheriff unlocked it. "You want to put me to work, eh?"

"For a fair day's wage, yes." Pecos pivoted around to hammer home his point. "I don't expect a man to work for free, not even if he's family."

"Well, now." Jones rubbed his dark hands together, as if carefully considering his request. "I might could stick around for a few days. Little Sis and I still have some catching up to do."

With a small shriek of delight, Meg took a running leap and threw herself into his arms. "Oh, Jones! I'm so happy you're going to stay in town for a spell."

"You think I'd let you get married without a brother to escort you down the aisle? No sirreee!" he chortled, swinging her around and around.

The marshal, who'd remained silent in the doorway up to this point, finally stepped into the room. "About your forthcoming nuptials, ma'am." He doffed his hat at her.

She glanced in his direction, looking mildly ill as Jones set her back on her feet. "Please don't ask of me what you're about to ask of me," she groaned.

Pecos' heart leaped at the realization she was as anxious to wed him as he was to wed her.

"Pray accept my apologies for any discomfort our arrangement has caused you." The marshal inclined his head. "However, I am closer than ever to making an arrest. If you would help me keep up appearances just a few days longer, I'd be most grateful."

When Meg hesitated, Thatcher Mills was quick to add, "If you help me put Redwood behind bars, you'll be saving countless young women a world of trouble."

"Well, how can I say no to that?" she sighed. With a long-suffering glance at Pecos, she gratefully thrust her slender arms into the fur coat he was holding up for her. "It's no trouble at all, Marshal. Why, at the rate we're going, Pecos and I should be wed a good few days shy of turning old and gray."

Thatcher Mills looked so sheepish that Pecos almost felt sorry for him. Almost. The man was brazenly holding up their marriage to work a case, and he knew it.

Jones had been huddled head-to-head with Jesse's father, muttering in undertones the whole time Pecos had been talking to the marshal. He straightened abruptly without turning around. "If I offer to perform the masonry work and keep the firewood stocked, might I be allowed to build a fireplace in here?"

The sheriff scowled at his shoulder blades. "For the record, our biggest objective here at the jailhouse is *not* to keep our prisoners in comfort."

Jones shrugged. "Well, if it's granting them an early release from jail by freezing them to death, then far be it from me to offer my free masonry services." He drew himself up, looking highly offended. "May your suffering be short, my friend," he tossed mockingly over his shoulder to Mr. Hawling, "seeing as how you're not long for this world." He ended his doomsday forecast with a blistering glare at the sheriff.

"Fine." Sheriff Rick Dawson snorted. "I wouldn't think of depriving my prisoner of his suffering. I'll expect you back in the morning, Jones Storm, with a bucket of cement and a pile of bricks."

Giving Mr. Hawling a two-fingered salute, Jones sauntered from the jailhouse, whistling merrily.

Meg hurried after him. "You have a kind heart, Jones. One you try to hide behind all that crust, but I know better."

"Whoa!" He held up one dark finger. "I have a reputation of hardness to maintain. Pray don't ruin it by gushing like a waterfall every time we are in public."

She rolled her eyes and all but skipped ahead of him to

the pair of horses Pecos had tethered to the hitching post. A happy sound escaped her to see he'd brought Midnight and Paint along, her two favorite horses.

"I've missed you," she crooned, patting their noses and resting her head briefly against theirs.

"No more than I've missed you." Pecos lifted her astride Paint and leaped up behind her. With a quick glance around them to ensure there were no loiterers behind the jail, he tipped her over his arm and dove in for a kiss.

He adored the small sound of surrender she made and the way her arms slid trustingly around his neck.

"Egads! It's a good thing I got a job at the jail," Jones noted sarcastically. "Otherwise, I'd have to witness you slobbering all over each other night and day."

"The job I'm offering you pays better," Pecos reminded. He tugged his affianced upright and hooked an arm around her waist to anchor her against his chest.

When his words were met with silence, he glanced over at Jones to find him staring in consternation at Midnight. "How do you expect me to ride this beast without a saddle?"

Pecos shrugged. He'd not been expecting to supply Jones with a horse, which is why he'd not come better prepared. "You just hop on and ride, brother."

Jones glanced over at the two of them, shaking his head and grumbling beneath his breath. "Here goes nothing, you big beast." He wrapped one long arm around Midnight's neck, then hoisted himself atop the enormous creature.

Midnight gave a short whinny of protest as he registered the sound, scent, and feel of a brand new rider.

"Easy, boy." Jones cautiously patted the horse's neck. "It's just a big ol' black man on a big ol' black horse."

Midnight trumped out another whinny and reared back on his hind legs, pawing the air.

"Why, you jack-a-napes, you!" Jones sputtered, clamping

his long legs around the horse's flanks and fisting both hands in the creature's mane.

Pecos was both surprised and pleased when Midnight quickly brought his heels back to the ground without unseating Jones.

As Jones fought to catch his breath, he shot a dark look at Pecos.

Pecos nodded at him. "That's how you do it."

Jones grumbled something else beneath his breath, but a twinkle lit his ebony gaze. "Lead the way, you loco chief."

PECOS HAD TO MOVE NIGHT FLYER AND SANKO INTO THE same cavern room, which neither minded, to temporarily install his future brother-in-law in his own guest chamber.

While Meg fluttered around the room, smoothing fur blankets and checking the oil level in the lantern, Jones nodded in satisfaction. "This is nice." He rubbed his hands briskly together and blew on them. "Much better than sleeping under the stars in the dead of winter." He gave a rueful huff. "And much warmer, even without the fire lit."

Pecos eyed the man's bare hands. "You'll be needing gloves to work outside."

"Bah!" Jones shrugged offhandedly. "I never use 'em."

A warning look from Meg told Pecos it was a sensitive topic. However, he had no intention of bowing to the fellow's pride and risking his fingers being eaten away by frost bite.

"It's part of our work uniform," he informed Jones, hoping to sound offhand. He signed a message to Night Flyer, who was nosily watching them in the doorway.

The teenager took off at a jog and returned a few minutes later with a sizable pile of supplies. He dumped them unceremoniously on the platform where Jones would be sleeping.

There were buckskin leggings that could be adjusted in or out at the waistline with a drawstring rope, an oversized tunic, and a massive fur coat. They were items that had once belonged to a Comanche elder, a man who'd passed two winters earlier.

Pecos calmly met Jones' defensive gaze. "They are not new, but they will keep you from feeling the fangs of winter."

Jones experimentally fingered the buckskin fabric. "I'll repay you as soon as I am able."

"That will not be necessary. As I said before," Pecos lied, "they are part of your uniform here at our mountain rodeo in the making." They weren't, of course. He hadn't given the first thought to an official uniform for his rodeo employees.

Jones changed from his tattered clothing to his borrowed togs in nothing flat and rejoined Pecos and Meg outdoors. Pecos was amused to see that he'd kept his black leather Stetson on. However, he'd rustled up a turkey feather and stuck it in the braided cord above the brim. He'd also forgone the moccasins Night Flyer had provided in lieu of keeping on his boots. The result was something that Pecos soon came to realize was distinctly Jones — a dandifed look to match the natural jaunt in his step.

Most importantly, Jones turned out to be a hard worker. For the next several days, he labored like a thousand demons were driving him. He awoke early to ride to the jail-house in town, where he spent the first few hours of each day building the fireplace he'd promised. Then he returned to the mountain in time to break his fast with Meg and Pecos.

Dakota served up bowls of piping hot cereal from his large hollowed-out cooking log. He kept the food warm by dropping glowing rocks in it from the nearby fire.

Though Pecos was anxious to make Meg his wife, he enjoyed every meal they shared together, every conversation, and every kiss. Her sweet loving warmed him from the inside out during the quickly falling temperatures.

His white-capped mountains provided the perfect backdrop for courting. Every day he fell more in love with her, and every day he grew one wall or room closer to building her the home she'd never had, the home where he would love and cherish her until the end of his days.

But first, there was something he needed to give her. He reached inside the leather pouch strung across his tunic and took out the granite ring he'd been whittling for the past week. He held it out to her. "I made this for you."

"Uh!" she breathed, her dark eyes lighting in appreciation. "It's so lovely." She tipped her head sideways to get a closer look at the tiny wolf he'd etched into the face of it. "You did all of this for me?"

"Yes. I wanted you to have a wedding ring."

She eyed it wistfully. "Do you want me to wait until we are wed to wear it?"

"No. I want you to wear it now. It is my promise to you that I will give you my name and hand. Soon."

Pink blossomed in her cheeks. "I will gladly wear your promise, Pecos — on my hand as well as in my heart." She pulled off her glove and held out her hand to him.

He gently slid the cold piece of granite on her finger, thrilled to find that it fit.

"I only wish I had something to give to you in return," she murmured, turning her hand this way and that to admire the ring.

"You do have something to give me," he countered, reaching out to draw a finger down her cheek. It was something he'd been wanting to ask her for days; he'd simply been waiting for the right moment. "Something that would mean far more to me than a trinket."

"Indeed?" She shyly scanned his features.

"I was hoping you would teach Night Flyer to read and write." He toyed with her fingers. "He has no ma, and there aren't any schools in town." *Yet.* He had a dream of helping to build one someday. There weren't many young folks in town to fill it yet, either.

"Of course I will, Pecos." She smiled adoringly at him. "I would welcome the chance to feel useful again."

Though her ankle was mostly healed, Pecos has been balking at the idea of her returning to the Christmas Mountain Inn. He wanted more time for word to circulate that there was no longer a bounty on her lovely head. The selfish part of him had also not been in a terrible hurry to share her again with the Remingtons. He liked having her all to himself. Or mostly to himself.

Jones's shadow fell over them as he crouched down beside the bonfire. "Morning, love birds!"

"You're back!" Meg happily waved her new ring at him. "Look what Pecos made me."

To Pecos' surprise, Jones sobered at the sight of the gift, then glanced off into the fire.

"Is everything alright?" Meg asked quickly. She tugged her glove back over her hand, hiding the ring.

"No. Not really."

"What can we do to help?" Pecos beat back a stab of disappointment, knowing this wasn't going to be a quick conversation. His special moment alone with Meg was over.

Jones snorted. "That attitude of yours." He waved a finger at Pecos. "It's what I'm struggling with this morning. You're always helping people for no reason at all. I don't understand it."

Meg reached over to squeeze his arm. "Says the big-hearted fellow who just finished building a fireplace for the sheriff's office for free."

He shrugged. "It's just a fireplace for a friend, but you..."

He scowled at Pecos. "You're building a whole blasted rodeo, and you're doing it for a town that ain't exactly welcomed you with open arms." He huffed out a breath. "Word on the street has it there are folks trying to take your land away from you as we speak. But here you are." He spread his hands. "Clearing trees and moving hills to construct a dad-gum racetrack for those same ungrateful wretches. Why?"

Pecos pondered his words for a moment, satisfied at the knowledge that the racetrack Jones was crabbing about would be finished by Christmas. "You're right. There are folks who aren't too fond of Comanche Falls that would like to take what's mine and have me carted off to a reservation." He glanced tenderly down at Meg. "But I have my reasons for wanting to stay and hold my ground."

"Right." Jones sounded glum. "You're in love with my sister."

"That's part of it. A big part of it, actually," Pecos agreed, reaching over to tuck a wisp of Meg's dark hair behind her ear. "But I made my decision long before she came into town."

"Again, why?" Jones demanded.

Pecos spread his hands. "Because I have a choice every morning. I can live the way a lot of my fellow citizens do and return evil for good. I could cut corners. I could cheat. I could steal. I could overcharge them for my horses. But all that would do is make me as evil as them." He grunted. "Or I could just be human and return evil for evil. An eye for an eye and a tooth for a tooth. When someone hurts me or mine, I could get revenge in the dead of night and leave no trail for them to follow. But all that would do is balance the scales. Fortunately, there's a third option, one I learned at the knees of a Godly mother."

"Must be nice." Jones sniffed. "I don't even remember my mother."

"I am sorry to hear it." Pecos could sense the sadness in him, along with the bitterness and weariness. "The third option is to spread goodness all the time — to return the goodness of others with goodness, and to return the evil of others with yet more goodness. Now that, my friend, is the way to truly make a difference in the world."

Jones shook his head. "So that's your secret? Be kind to everyone, even to those who are unkind to you?"

"Someone has to be the first." Pecos reached around Meg to clap him on the shoulder. "I know it doesn't make sense, but it's what the Bible tells us to do. What's more, it really works." When Edward had spread the word about the new rodeo the Comanches had under construction, the petition about the land auction had died a quick and natural death.

Jones remained squatting, but he bowed his head over his clasped hands. "I reckon I'm just tired. I'm tired of being angry. Tired of dealing with all the folks who take one look at the color of my skin and don't want to give me a fair shot at anything. I'm plumb worn out with it all."

Meg sucked in an anxious breath and leaned closer to him to rest her head against his arm. "Would you like us to pray with you?"

"Yes," he muttered. "I'm done trying to change the world. It's too big and too messed up. But maybe if God could change me so I could see things in a different light..."

"He can," she assured, her dark eyes glistening with adoration. "Pecos?" she whispered, beseeching him to join them.

He moved around them to crouch on the other side of Jones. "You're my family, Jones, and you're Meg's family. You know that, right?"

Jones nodded.

"You know you're welcome to stay here on the mountain as long as you want. Or for good."

Jones nodded again.

"But if you become a friend of God, you can take Him with you off this mountain, into town, across state lines, and everywhere you go. You'll never have to be alone again."

A large tear splashed on the ground between Jones's boots. "That's what I want," he cried hoarsely. "How do I get it?"

"By inviting God to come into your heart. By putting Him first above everything else in your life."

Jones nodded, and they began to pray together. At first, he only repeated the words that Pecos coaxed him to say, but eventually he came up with his own. "Help me to see the world as you see it, Lord. To see others the way you see them. To change the things I am able to change and to accept the things I cannot."

When he finally raised his head, his melancholy was gone. In its place was his old grin. Or a new one. Pecos had never quite seen the glint Jones was wearing in his eyes.

"Thank you." He bounded to his feet. "I feel like a new man, and I know what I need to do first."

"What is that?" Meg accepted Pecos' help to tug her to her feet.

"I want to get married."

"What?" she gasped.

Pecos stared. It was not the typical declaration a man made after deciding to follow Christ.

"Yes, indeed. I want it all, folks!" Jones crowed, backing away from the bonfire to do a little jig in the snow. "I want to be a better man, but why stop there? I also want a woman in my life who will love me as much as Meg loves you." Dancing his way across the clearing, he approached Midnight, who surprisingly held still while he leaped atop the creature's back.

"Where are you going?" Meg looked mystified.

"To pay Clink Redwood a visit." He grinned down at her.

"But he's a criminal!" she protested.

"Indeed, he is." Jones didn't look the least bit discouraged. "So I shall put my investigative skills to work and help out with the case. If I succeed, the two of you can be wed all the sooner, and I just might end up with a mail-order bride, myself."

Pecos watched him ride away, then spun Meg around in his arms. "Now, where were we before he interrupted us?"

She smoothed her hands over the furry fabric covering his shoulders. "I believe we were discussing Night Flyer's schooling."

"No, after that." He pulled her closer.

"You gave me a beautiful ring," she noted softly.

"Close enough." He lowered his head over hers. "This." His lips touched hers. "This is what I've been wanting to do all morning."

৩৯৩

JONES WAS STARTING TO LIKE RIDING BAREBACK. SHOOT! IT was nice riding at all — so much better than walking everywhere. He'd never owned a horse before. It was enough to make a man feel, well, like more of a man. Someone who was on top of the world instead of forever being trod beneath the feet of others.

And he planned to take that good feeling one step further this morning by signing a mail-order bride contract. Between what the sheriff had paid him for the fireplace and what Pecos had been paying him to clear his land for a horse track, he had a nice little nest egg growing. It was more than enough to help him sink his teeth into the Clink Redwood case. The beauty of it was that folks were always discounting his abilities on account of his skin color, so an outlaw like Clink would never see what was coming.

He'd forgotten to bring a rope to tether Midnight, so

when he arrived at the mail-order bride agency, he left the creature in front of the hitching post. "Stay," he ordered sternly.

Midnight nickered and started snuffling the ground.

"Good boy." Jones pushed open the front door. A bell attached to a string gave a little jingle to announce his arrival.

Clink Redwood was lounged at a desk in the center of the room, blowing smoke rings at the ceiling. At the sight of Jones, he didn't bother straightening in his seat, much less giving him the courtesy of standing. If anything, his tall, bony figure slouched farther down in his chair.

"Well?" he demanded rudely. His black suit hung so loosely on his frame that he looked downright skeletal.

"I'm in the market for a wife," Jones announced cheerily, ignoring the fellow's scowl of disapproval.

"I'm not certain I know how to acquire what you're looking for." Clink surveyed him with dreary eyes. His white hair was standing on end, as if he'd been running his hand through it.

Jones could practically taste his agitation. "What?" He pretended astonishment as he dug in his pocket and produced a wad of dollar bills. "I was certain I saw a sign out front that indicated you were running a bridal agency. If I was mistaken, pray accept my apologies while I take my business elsewhere."

Mr. Redwood gave a loud harrumph and finally sat up straight, his gray eyes glued on the money Jones was idly counting in the air. "Yes, I run a bridal agency. Aren't you the fellow who just got out of jail? And where in the world did you get all that money?"

"From the men who pay my salary. My little overnight stay in the jailhouse was just a big misunderstanding," Jones returned loftily. He paused his counting. "You know how it is with these trigger-happy cowboys in small towns." He figured talking down the law might give them some common ground.

Clink snickered. "You sound just like my investor friends."

Investors, eh? Jones fixed him with a half-curious, half-amused stare.

The matchmaker waved a hand. "Big city fellows," he bragged. "One's an attorney who has absolutely no patience with these small-town lawmen."

An attorney. Check. Keep talking your way into a hole, mister. Soon you'll be in so deep, there will be no way out. He abruptly changed the subject to keep the fellow off balance. Still counting out bills, he mused, "I take it the bridal business isn't all that profitable in a town this size, eh? Hence your need to expand into other markets." He infused as much sympathy into his voice as he could.

"You guessed it." The matchmaker adopted a superior tone, waving a finger. "As a matter of fact, I have a big payday coming. A real big payday." He puffed out his chest.

"I'm glad to hear it." Jones' suspicions were immediately roused. As he glanced around, he could see nothing in Mr. Redwood's spare little office that suggested a big payday was on the horizon. The room was dusty and devoid of all furniture besides his desk. From what he could gather, the man had only successfully married off two brides in all of Christmas Mountain.

The matchmaker followed his gaze. "I know it doesn't look like much, but I have friends in high places."

"Lucky you." Jones resumed counting his cash, enjoying the hungry look that leaped into the man's face. Regardless of any big payday he had looming, he was clearly strapped for funds at the moment. Jones would bet his eye teeth on that fact. However, he didn't rush to dig for more information. He'd learned the power of both sound and silence a long time ago — how to say just enough to keep the other fellow talking and how to say little enough to make him rush to fill the awkward silence.

Clink lowered his voice, even though they were the only two people in the building. "Well, seeing as you have money to pay up front, I...ah, might could match you up with one of the señoritas we have coming to town." He glanced furtively around them. "These friends of mine have hit big times. They deal with lots more brides than I do, which is why I doubt they'd mind too much if you and I were to strike a deal right here and now for one of them." He leaned forward and started pushing papers around his desk.

Clink Redwood's words rushed past Jones' brain, creating an alarming picture. *Big city fellows. Big payday coming. Señoritas. Lots more brides. Strike a deal right here and now for one...* The details could add up to only one conclusion: The man had to be referring to the trafficking of women from Mexico. Jones' heart sang in unholy delight, and he mentally prepared to report his findings to the marshal. *Oh, Mr. Thatcher Mills, sir. I think I just busted your case wide open. You want to arrest ol' Clink Redwood? This is how you do it.*

It was simply a matter of finding out the when and the how, so Clink could be caught red-handed — him and all his cronies alike.

"So, ah..." Jones continued counting money in the air. "How soon can you guarantee the delivery of my sweet little *señorita?*"

"Well, it depends." Clink licked his dry lips.

Jones half-turned toward the door. "I prefer to do business with folks who can provide guarantees."

"Very well. I can have her here next week," the matchmaker blurted. "On Thursday."

Jones chuckled. "That's Christmas Eve." It was the same day as the first rodeo Pecos would be hosting. Not all of the rodeo facilities would be fully constructed by then, but the stables would be. So would the race track and at least one of the performance rings.

"I can think of no better holiday gift for a man, if you know what I mean." Clink leered suggestively at him.

Jones was afraid he very much knew what the man meant. His blood ran ten angry shades of hot just thinking about it. "How might I go about getting in touch with your friends?"

"You don't!" Clink looked horrified. "That's my job. All you do is pay the money, and I deliver the bride."

"You're making this too easy, sir. I think we have ourselves a deal." Jones drenched him with a mile-wide grin. "I'm willing to pay half now and half at delivery. If she's pretty, I'll be sure to throw in a little extra." He peeled off a few bills and moved toward the man's desk with purpose, stretching out his arm to set them down. At the last second, however, he snatched the bills back. "Wait! I almost forgot."

Clink's eyes stayed on the money. "What is it?"

"Paperwork. I don't usually hand over money to a fellow without having him first write me out a receipt."

"Of course." The matchmaker shoved more papers around his desk, knocked over his inkwell, and set it back upright. Fortunately, the cap remained intact. Otherwise, it would have made a terrible mess.

While the man hastily wrote out a receipt, Jones hovered, reading every item on his desk he could put his eyeballs on. At one point, he pretended to lean on the desk, just so he could knock around a few more papers.

He caught a glimpse of a calendar with the last several days checked off. There was a big circle around the block representing next Thursday. More than likely, that was when the next delivery of women would take place, which was why that was the day Clink said he could deliver Jones' *señorita*. He also saw the stub of a train ticket, as well as the name Hildebrand scratched on a piece of paper. No surprise there. About a year ago, Iris Hildebrand, Jesse Hawling's wife, had passed through this office as a mail-order bride. His brain swam with the other details he'd gathered, sorting them and trying to make sense of them. *Border crimes. Trains. Señoritas. Thursday. Investors. Big payday.*

The moment Clink handed him the hastily scrawled receipt, Jones slapped the money into his outreached palm. "I'll be back with the rest of it on Thursday," he lied, pivoting to face the door. He fully planned to be shadowing Clink Redwood's every move between now and Thursday. Hopefully, the sheriff and a few deputies would be willing to join him in his efforts.

"I look forward to doing business with you," the matchmaker called after him.

I'm sure you do. Jones waved without turning around and breezed out of the building.

CHAPTER 10: SHOWDOWN
JONES

J ones headed straight for the sheriff's office. Well, in a round about way, at least. He had Midnight retrace his steps a few times in the alley behind Main Street to ensure he hadn't been followed. Then he crept to the station from the rear and leaped from his horse.

"Stay," he ordered, trying to mimic the low, rumbly voice Pecos used when he was in the training ring. The man sure knew how to talk to his horses, and Jones believed in learning a thing or two from the best. He took a moment to smooth a hand over the horse's nose, something else Pecos always did. "You're doing a great job today, fella. Keep it up, and you'll have a treat waiting for you back at the stables."

The new stables on Pecos Carlson's land boasted no frills. They were basic, saltbox buildings that didn't even have a coat of paint on them yet. Pecos kept saying it was too cold outside to paint just yet. However, the stables were well-built and sturdy, thanks to all the Comanches who'd been swinging hammers lately. Jones never had a pa in his life to pass down such skills. However, he'd been swinging a hammer right alongside them, and they seemed to appreciate the brute strength he added to the mix.

"I thought I heard something out here!" Sheriff Rick Dawson poked his uncovered head out the back door, allowing the December wind to lift the auburn waves from his forehead. "What brings you back to town, Jones? I thought you finished the fireplace two days ago."

"Business," Jones retorted flatly. He glanced around them. "May we take this conversation inside?"

"Of course." Rick Dawson pushed the door wider, eyeing him with curiosity.

"Any chance you've laid eyes on Thatcher Mills today?" Jones stomped the snow off his boots as he mounted the stairs and stepped inside the small office. There were two deputies hunched over their desks, and the man in question was pacing in front of them. "Never you mind. I see the badge in question."

Thatcher glanced up as he approached. "Well, howdy, Jones!" Despite his friendly greeting, he looked weary — like a man who was long overdue for a bit of good news, and Jones had it to share in spades.

The wood-burning stove was belching out untold amounts of heat. He unbuttoned his fur "uniform" coat from Pecos to avoid roasting to death inside of it. "Not to brag, but I just solved your case for you, marshal."

"If only." Thatcher ran a hand over his short blonde hair. "My wife said if I wasn't home by Christmas to not bother coming back. She's in the family way," he explained with a disheartened groan. "Unfortunately, this case has failed to inch along at more than a snail's pace."

"Well, allow me to help you speed things up."

Thatcher stuffed his hands in his pockets with a long-suffering huff. "I'm all ears, Mr. Storm."

"Is that why you look like you want to hurt me?" Jones grinned.

"This is my anxious face. My anxious-to-hear-how-an-ex-bounty-hunter-accomplished-what-a-federal-marshal-could-not face."

Jones pretended to turn around and head for the door. "Pray forgive me. I don't have that kind of time to spare."

"I'm hanging on to my patience by a thread over here, Storm."

Hearing Thatcher drop the Mister made Jones grin wider. He spun around. "Since you asked so nicely, I'll tell you. I paid a visit to Clink Redwood."

"I didn't ask you to," the marshal shot back testily. "There's a thousand penalties I could slap on your cocky head for interfering in a federal case."

"Oh? I didn't realize I needed your permission to get married, Marshal."

Thatcher drew a deep breath. "Is that your real reason for interfering with my case?"

"One of them, at least," Jones retorted cheerfully. "My biggest reason is I'm sick and tired of Pecos and Meg moping up one side of the mountain and down the other. They need to be wed, Marshal, which means this case needs to be wrapped up pronto! My second biggest reason for visiting Clink was because I am sorely jealous of all their turtledove billing and cooing and, in fact, *do* wish to marry."

Thatcher pulled his hands out of his pockets to spread them in the air. "You're a troublemaker, Storm. Anyone can spot that a mile away, but you have my attention."

Good. Jones turned deadly serious. When it came to bringing criminals to justice, he didn't play around. "Our illustrious local matchmaker claims to have big city friends. One is an attorney. Both are investors. Both also are involved in the business of placing young women into the arms of men who are willing to pay for them. *Señoritas* was the exact word he used. Lots of them." He rattled off the information he'd tucked into his unfailing memory with the precision of a soldier. "Somehow, Redwood managed to get these same friends to cut him in on a deal involving a large payout. Some of the items I saw on his desk were as follows: A calendar with next Thursday circled, a train ticket stub, and no fresh bridal contracts or coffee mug rings. That means Ol' Clink hasn't spent much time lately matching brides with grooms. I'm not sure that a federal marshal like yourself would consider that to be a case breaking clue, but bounty hunters like myself don't overlook even the smallest of details."

"Watch it there, Storm." Thatcher shook his head in warning, but Jones could tell he was only trying to hide just how vigorously he was hanging on to every word of his report.

He jumped into the final part of his report. "I happen to find Clink's lack of matchmaking lately particularly interesting, since he claims he's running a mail-order bride agency. I paid half down for my *señorita* today, and I demanded a receipt in return, so you'd have a legally obtained sample of his handwriting. Here it is." He tossed it on the sheriff's desk. "I'm to pay the other half at delivery and a little extra if she's pretty." Jones slapped one large black hand atop the paper. "You only need to be there to make the arrest when he hands over a trafficked woman to me."

Thatcher stopped his pacing and sank heavily into the wooden chair parked beside the sheriff's desk. "As much as I hate to reward such a display of insufferable cockiness, I have to hand it to you, Mr. Storm. You cracked our case wide open." He shook his head in disbelief. "Please assure me you connected the same dots I did, Sheriff Dawson."

Rick Dawson nodded grimly. He'd been scratching notes on a piece of paper while Jones spoke. "We can tell you exactly who those big city investors are. Penn Remington and Fargus Hildebrand. For the longest time, I couldn't make heads or tails out of why Penn was lingering in town. All I know is he and his younger son, Edward, don't rub along too well. But what if his presence in town had nothing to do with Edward? What if that was just a convenient cover story? What if he's actually here to hustle women from the border?"

Jones wasn't certain who Penn Remington or Fargus Hildebrand were, but he narrowed his gaze on the sheriff, carefully processing the information he was so generously sharing.

The marshal thoughtfully stroked his chin. "That would certainly explain why Remington, Senior was the one heading the petition to auction off Pecos Carlson's land. It would also explain why he paid a visit to the mayor today with a huge donation to his re-election campaign, along with a request to immediately reopen the petition. All we need to figure out now is what's located in Comanche territory that he wants so badly?"

Jones shrugged. "Mountains, foothills, caves, canyons, valleys, and mounds of snow."

Rick Dawson waggled a finger. "There's also an abandoned train depot plus a railroad spur that was abandoned years ago." He slapped his hands on his desk as a thought struck him, half rising to his feet. "Any chance it's still operable?"

"It might be. There's only one way to find out for sure." The marshal stood. "We need to explore every square inch of that mountain, scour every trail, and turn over every stone."

"And we only have four days to do it before Christmas Eve," Jones pointed out. "I imagine Pecos and his tribe will do everything they can to assist us, but keep in mind that's the same day they'll be hosting their first rodeo. No doubt they'll be thrilled to find out their bronc riding events on the north side of their property will be happening at the same time as the women trafficking hand-off on the south side." He was inwardly livid about Penn Remington's stubborn pursuit of auctioning off the Comanche's land. *Over my dead body, you greedy, grasping buzzard! You just messed with the wrong family.* Pecos was the only person in the world besides Meg who'd ever called him family. And he didn't just call Jones family, he treated him like family.

Sheriff Dawson clapped on his Stetson. "At least the rodeo will give us lawmen the perfect excuse to be present. I intend to have a jolly good time watching the races and an even jollier time rounding ourselves up a pack of outlaws."

"That's the spirit!" Thatcher Mills heartily clapped his hands. "I do believe you fellas may have just saved my marriage. It'll be cutting it close, but there's a sliver of a chance I'll make it home for Christmas, after all."

"Jones Storm." The sheriff folded his arms and pivoted to face Jones squarely. "I can't believe what I'm about to say. But if you're in no hurry to leave town after this case is closed, I could sorely use another deputy."

"Me?" Jones pointed at his chest, wondering if there was something wrong with his ears. *You want to pin a badge on a black man?*

The sheriff's smile disappeared. "The truth is, I haven't had the heart to replace Jesse Hawling yet. I just keep borrowing deputies from the next county over," he waved his hand at the two men currently holding down desks in the room, "and hoping and praying he'll return. But you're what the Lord sent my way."

Jones' heart sang at the thought of becoming a lawman. "If your offer is a serious one, I'd be honored, sir." *Look at me, about to get all deputized!* A poor black man who'd gotten his start in an orphanage, no less. *Yes, sirreee! I'm moving up in the world, folks.*

"It's a serious offer, Mr. Storm, take it or leave it."

"I'm taking it, sir."

"Good." Rick Dawson thrust out a hand, looking bemused. "It's been a whole blasted year. I reckon Jesse Hawling's not ever coming back. And even if he does, I'd be lying if I didn't say there's enough work in this town for two full-time deputies."

Jones clasped his hand, grinning widely. *Good, because you might just end up with two before this is all over.*

⊗⊗

THE DAY OF THE RODEO DAWNED ICY BUT CLEAR. PECOS rose at first light, anxious to commence his final checklist of tasks. He still couldn't believe how much support the townsmen of Christmas Mountain were giving the event. Both Edward and Mav had been present. Even the town sheriff and his ever-growing posse of deputies had spent the last four days helping out from dawn until dusk. Sure, they were working their case, but they'd done an awful lot of helping out with the rodeo preparations, too.

Pecos held up his lantern as he marched silently between the stalls of his newest boarding stable. Exactly twenty-one Mustangs were rowed up, ten on one side and eleven on the other. There were nine empty stalls remaining and another thirty empty ones in the other stable next door. It had taken many hours of back-breaking labor, but he couldn't have been prouder of the work his fellow Comanches had performed. The race track and one horse ring were complete, as well, and they had plans to keep building. There were more rings to complete and guest stands to erect. However, that would have to wait until next spring, possibly even next summer.

His crew was currently hard at work building the house he planned to gift to Meg on their wedding day. Afterward, they would commence construction on a set of log cabins for the rest of his tribe. He could probably coax the younger Natives to move into the cabins. Most of the elders would probably insist on remaining in the caverns, though, and that was alright, too.

He heard a feathery light footfall behind him and instantly knew who it was. "Two Dark Moons." He spun around but was greeted by an empty hallway. That was odd. He was certain he'd heard the delicate footstep of a female. Puzzled, he returned his attention to the horses.

"You're the stars of today's show." He monologued to them in a low voice. He pointed at the pair in the first stall. "You two will give pony rides." He kept moving down the aisle, pointing and talking. "And you five will buck the living daylights out of all the fools who think they can ride a bronc." Sanko and his team of range riders would be out on patrol throughout the entire event. Every horse would have its mission today.

Lord willing, the sheriff would finally succeed in rounding up Clink Redwood and the outlaws he was in cahoots with today. Pecos' heart thumped in anticipation, knowing it would allow him to marry the woman who owned his heart at long last.

"Pecos?" a soft, musical voice called.

Two Dark Moons! This time, he was not imagining her presence. The angel who haunted every one of his dreams was truly in the stable. He held up his lantern, watching her make her way toward him.

She had never looked more beautiful to him than she did in the flickering lantern light. She was wearing the cozy buckskin tunic and leggings he'd gifted her, along with the bear fur coat. However, her dark hair, which had been pulled up in a complicated twist the first day he met her, was styled differently this morning. He was utterly enchanted by the two glossy braids hanging over her slender shoulders. Though she did not share his Native blood, she'd proven to be the perfect maiden for a tribal chief — the perfect bride for him.

"Why are you looking at me like that?" she asked breathlessly, as she came to stand before him.

"Because you are a gift from Heaven. Because your eyes are shining at me like two dark, glorious moons. Because you are so lovely, I'll never finish looking my fill of you — not in ten moons or fifty." He bent his knees to set the lantern on the floor. Then he held out his arms to her.

She stepped into them. "I love you so much, Pecos! I—"

"Pray forgive the intrusion." Jones Storm's mocking voice swept through the stable, shattering the sweetness of the moment.

"Ugh!" Meg muttered, resting her forehead against his shoulder. "My brother is forever popping up at the most importune times."

"Ah. There you are, sis," Jones noted gleefully, ignoring the fact that she was wrapped securely in Pecos' arms. "I thought I saw you walk this way and figured you could use a hand with your morning chores."

"Your heart is bigger than your body," she noted sarcastically, "which is saying a lot, since you're a giant pain in my backside—"

A decidedly feminine sneeze interrupted her sisterly tirade. The three of them turned in the direction of the sound and found themselves staring in astonishment at one of the empty horse stalls.

The first streaks of sunlight were pushing their way across the sky, brightening the windows with a warm glow.

"I'll handle this." Jones strode to the stall and pushed open the door.

"Jones, don't," Meg pleaded. "You have no idea what's on the other side of that wall."

OH, YES, I DO. IT'S A WOMAN, OR MY NAME'S NOT—

"Jumping Jehoshaphat!" he exclaimed, staring at the slender figure huddled in rags in the corner of the hay. Her teeth were chattering, and she was shivering uncontrollably.

Yanking off his fur coat, he hurried forward, fully intending to toss it around her shoulders. However, she shrank away from him with a piteous moan. Fear darkened her coffee bean eyes, and she looked about ready to swoon.

Knowing he probably resembled a big, hulking beast in the dim light, he crouched down in front of her, careful to keep back a few feet.

"I'm not going to hurt you." He held out his coat to her. "You're cold. You need this more than me."

Pecos and Meg caught up to him.

"Oh, Jones!" His sister thrust the lantern into the stall. "She's terrified. Here. Let me." She swiftly traded him the lantern for the coat. Inching toward the woman, she gently draped the fur around her shoulders. "There," she murmured softly. "This will chase away the chill."

"*Gracias.*" The young woman gave a violent shiver. "Th-thank you."

"You speak English!" Meg noted in delight. She remained stooped in front of the woman.

"A l-little."

"Fantastic!" Meg clasped her hands in front of her. "Because I speak no Spanish. Do either of you?" She shot a curious glance over her shoulder at Pecos and Jones.

"Some," Jones admitted. "Enough to get by."

He watched as Meg attempted to assist the lovely Mexican woman to her feet, but she sank back to the floor of the stall with a keening sigh.

"So weak," she murmured. "Long t-time. No food."

Convinced that they'd found one of the trafficked *señoritas*, Jones was anxious to share the news with the sheriff and marshal on patrol outside. However, he was even more anxious to see to the comfort of the half-starved woman in front of him. His blood boiled at the thought of how many other women had been abused and neglected like this. He was going to take great joy in bringing the animals who'd done this to justice.

He held out a hand to her. "I'll carry you, ma'am, if you'll let me."

She shuddered as she eyed his large paw.

There was something about the abject defeat in her gaze that brought out every protective instinct in him. "Here." He reached for his pistol.

"What are you doing?" Meg gasped.

"Giving her back her dignity." He unsnapped his gun and removed it from his holster.

Tears of terror dripped down the curves of the *señorita's* cheeks as she watched him.

"Here." He laid the pistol on the floor and slowly slid it in her direction. "Take it. No one is ever going to hurt you again."

"Jones," Meg breathed. "I sure hope you know what you're doing."

"Me too, sis." He let go of the pistol and raised his hands in surrender.

She snatched it up with shaking fingers. However, all she did was clutch it to her chest, swaying dizzily.

"There, now," Jones said in his gentlest voice. "You're armed, and I'm not. Let me carry you, *amiga*." He held out his arms again. "*Las agua*," he promised. "*La comida*." They were the Spanish words for water and food.

More tears dripped down her face, but she nodded.

"Don't shoot," he pleaded in a whisper as he gently lifted

her into his arms. He was amazed at how delicate she felt, like a fragile little bird. It wasn't until her slender frame was clasped against his chest, however, that he noted her ball-shaped belly.

"*Por Dios!*" he muttered. She was with child.

The woman sagged against him, nearly dropping the pistol.

He caught it and returned it to his holster. "You're safe now. *A salvo,*" he repeated, in case she didn't understand the English word for safe.

She dropped her head weakly against his shoulder. "My n-name is *Mariana.*"

"Pleased to meet you, ma'am," he assured softly. "Jones Storm, at your service."

๑๖๕

ONCE MARIANA GOT A BIT OF DAKOTA'S HOT CEREAL warming her insides and was sipping on a mug of Meg's signature chamomile, she was more than anxious to tell her story.

To Jones' secret delight, she selected a seat near him at the Comanche bonfire, still bundled inside his coat.

They were gathered on the north side of Pecos' property, where all the newly constructed rodeo facilities were located. It was a good half-mile or so from their hidden cavern village. The bonfire was located at what Jones could only describe as a Native American town square. A short wall of stacked stone surrounded the wall, no more than two hands high, and a cluster of logs and boulders had been artfully arranged around it for seating.

Mariana was huddled atop an oversized boulder. However, she was sitting on the side where Jones was standing, close enough to reach out and touch his hand if she wanted. While she spoke, she kept darting curious, measuring glances up at him.

He watched her silently, trying not to think too hard about how silky her unbound dark hair looked, as it riffled around her shoulders in the morning breeze. Or how many emotions were flitting through her umber eyes. Or how kiss-able her pink petal lips appeared.

Down, boy! He tried to school his thoughts to a more professional channel, tried to look away from her and simply absorb the details of the case, but it was impossible. His gaze kept returning, of its own volition, to their lovely guest; so he focused his thoughts, instead, on the many unpleasant ways he was going to extract a confession of guilt from the men who had done this to her.

Her tale was one of heart wrenching tragedy and betrayal. She and a dozen other young Mexican women had been taken from the small border town of *Generoso*. Her husband had been promised a job in the mines there.

"It was lie," she spat. The faster she spoke, the more broken her English became. "All lie. No house. No pay. No keep promise. The mine collapse. All our men die." Angry tears streaked her sun-kissed face. "We hungry, cold, poor. When the *hombres* from the north come, we sign our X to become mail-order brides." She shook her head. "Still more lie. No food. No *agua*. No husband. Nothing but *infierno*," she spat.

Jones recognized that word all too well. Her existence had become a living hell. Though the young mother-to-be desper-ately needed rest, he ruthlessly plied her with more questions until Pecos stood and held up his hands to halt the inter-rogation.

"Enough. I know where the other women are being held, and I know just the man to take you there. I'd escort you there, myself, but I have a rodeo about to begin."

The townsfolk were already trickling in to spectate. Horses and buggies were already lining the hitching posts, and folks were already milling around the training ring, exclaiming over the Comanche's latest batch of Mustangs on display. The first bronc riding event would commence in less than an hour.

Pecos raised a hand to his lips and blew a few blasts of an eagle's cry.

There was an answering eagle cry. Then a man swaggered out from the nearest stable door. He strode up to those gathered around the bonfire and came to a halt in front of where Sheriff Rick Dawson was perched on a log. Giving him a mocking salute, he pushed back his Stetson. "I know it's been a while, sheriff, but this is Deputy Jesse Hawling, reporting for duty."

Rick Dawson grew as still as death for several seconds. Then he gave a whoop of joy so loud that it echoed off the surrounding canyon walls. He leaped to his feet to embrace the lawman he'd been so reluctant to replace.

"Providence is on our side, and justice will be served today. I can feel it in my bones." He turned to face the rest of them, with an arm still slung around Jesse. Catching Jones' gaze, the sheriff ordered, "Let's go round up some outlaws, boys!" He dug in his pocket and pulled out a shiny new deputy badge. "I brought this along just in case." He tossed it to Jones, who easily caught it in mid air. "Consider yourself deputized, Jones Storm. We'll be needing all hands on deck today."

Awe flooded Jones' chest at the approval and acceptance oozing from the sheriff. Either that, or he was a little giddy in the brain over the admiration shining in Mariana's eyes as she tipped her heart-shaped face up to him.

"God be with you," she intoned softly.

"He will," Jones assured huskily. His hand went automatically to his pistol. Unsnapping it from his holster as he'd done earlier, he handed it back to her. "Stay safe until I return, *bella*."

She shook her head vehemently, making her curtain of dark hair dance across her eyes. "No. You need it." She tried to shove the pistol back in his direction.

Holding her beautiful gaze, he slowly lifted his tunic to display the extra pair of pistols strapped to his midriff.

Her delighted peal of laughter surrounded him like music as she snatched the gun from his fingers. Then she stood and unwound his coat from her shoulders. "Stay warm until you return, Jones Storm."

⊱✦⊰

Thanks to Mariana's timely escape and the intelligence she was able to provide about her captors, the ambush the sheriff and his men engineered took blessedly little time to set in place. They reached the cavern she'd described in less than ten minutes. It was located just outside the abandoned train depot. Clink Redwood, himself, was lounged in front of its entrance, leaning back against the rocky wall and puffing rings of smoke into the sky. His rifle was lying idly against his shoulder, while his cigar got most of his attention.

Sheriff Dawson gave a set of silent commands via hand signals, and their posse of lawmen obediently scattered and took up their positions. Deputies Storm and Hawling stealthily closed in on him from behind to cover the east side of the cavern entrance. The deputies on loan from the adjacent county moved in to cover the west side of the entrance. Marshal Thatcher Mills low-crawled his way through the tall, dead grass to anchor the center of their formation. He was an expert marksman. No one would be getting past his crossfire.

As soon as everyone was in position, Rick Dawson gave the agreed-upon signal, the short screech of a hawk.

While Clink's head jerked heavenward in search of the bird, Jones and Jesse moved in and laid him out cold on the ground without firing a shot. After securing his hands and feet and stuffing an old rag in his mouth to keep him silent when he awoke, they removed him from the cavern entrance and dumped him in the underbrush.

A full twenty minutes passed before the next man poked his head outside the cavern. Jones had never seen him before, but he recognized him from his description. It was Fargus Hildebrand, Iris Hawling's unscrupulous uncle who'd caused her and Jesse so much heartache. Unfortunately, Jones and Jesse were too far away to nab him, since they'd just finished securing Clink's still form. The sheriff and his borrowed deputies, however, were ready. They made short work of the second outlaw, rendering him unconscious with the butt of a pistol.

Jones and Jesse returned to their previous position and fanned out, one on either side of the cavern entrance, while the sheriff and his other deputies tied up Hildebrand and dragged him over to where the matchmaker was laid out.

The whimper of a female in pain nearly proved to be Jones' undoing. Acting on sheer instinct, he drew his pistol and leaped in front of the cavern entrance.

None other than Penn Remington emerged next, but he wasn't alone. A writhing, sobbing *señorita* was in his grasp. Mr. Remington held her carefully in front of him with a pistol pressed against her temple.

"My lands!" Jones shook his head at the aging attorney, too furious to be afraid. "This isn't going to end well, but I think you already know that. You really shoulda stuck to lawyering."

The pistol in Mr. Remington's hand trembled. "How do you know who I am?"

"Everybody is about to know who you are," Jones mocked. He needed to keep the man talking long enough for Jesse to make his move. But, by George, he was thoroughly enjoying the opportunity to provoke this particular *hombre*. "The name Penn Remington is going to be plastered across every newspaper from the East Coast to the West Coast when this dark-as-sin cowboy is done slapping your lily-white hands in cuffs."

"Drop your gun," the attorney snarled, removing his pistol from the woman's head and training it in Jones' direction. If it weren't for the weapon in his hands, he might've passed for a debonaire gentleman of leisure. His pinstriped wool suit and black overcoat appeared to be richly tailored. Jones had a weakness for nice apparel; though he'd never been able to afford it, he'd often window shopped. That's how he knew the man's black top hat was also of the highest quality. Alas, his heart was far blacker than the color of Jones' skin. All of this, he determined in the swiftest of seconds.

"Alright, alright. If you insist." He hastily lowered his pistol to the ground. He wasn't about to pick a fight with the barrel of a gun. But, mercy! He hoped Jesse hopped into the fray soon. Otherwise, Jones wasn't going to get to enjoy attending his first rodeo, after all. Or being around long enough to court a certain *señorita*.

In that moment, the sobbing woman wrenched free of Penn Remington's grasp. During the brief lull in which he took his gaze off of Jones and stared after her, Jesse stepped forward and wrenched the man's pistol away.

"On your knees, Remington," he ordered coldly.

The attorney took one look at who was doing the talking and paled. "Just shoot me now, Deputy Hawling. You know you want to."

"In your dreams, city slicker." Jesse gave an unholy

chuckle that held no mirth. "What I really want to see is you on your knees. And don't expect any help from your son. More than likely, he'll be representing all the lovely ladies you stole from their homes."

Mr. Remington slowly slid to his knees in the snow. "We did them a favor," he snarled. "Those women were nothing. Less than nothing after the mine collapsed. We were their ticket out of poverty."

Jones stooped to retrieve his pistol. "What do you know about poverty, mister?" He shook his head in derision. "No. Don't answer that question. I will. You don't know the first thing about poverty, but you're going to learn all about it from behind the bars of a jail cell."

"That'll never happen," the older man bellowed, turning red. "I have powerful connections from coast to coast. No judge will believe the word of some two-bit cowboy posing as a—"

"Maybe not, Mr. Remington, but they'll listen to me." The marshal rose from his position in the tall grass, holding up his badge. "We've never met, but I'm U.S. Marshal Thatcher Mills..."

⚜

RICK DAWSON ORDERED HIS EXTRA DEPUTIES TO ROUND UP the other two prisoners. He left Jones Storm in charge of the newly rescued *señoritas* inside the cavern, with the promise that he'd send food, water, and blankets to them within the hour. It was going to be an enormous task sorting out all of their identities and returning them to their loved ones where they belonged. The sheriff, however, was determined to see to their immediate welfare and comfort first. The paperwork and administrative details could come later.

Their remaining posse of lawmen made the short march

back with their three prisoners to where their collection of wagons was parked. By the time they arrived, the rodeo was in full swing.

Jesse Hawling took extraordinary pleasure in marching the handcuffed Penn Remington past the milling crowd of guests — right up to the point where he caught sight of Edward Remington's pale face and pained gaze. The innkeeper was standing outside the horse ring with one arm draped around Lacey's shoulders. She was decked out in a new winter cloak dripping with seed pearls, a blushing bride very much in love with the husband she was gazing up at.

That was when Jesse realized there'd be no joy in this arrest, after all. Justice had come full circle. This is what had to happen — the only thing that could've ever bought his and Iris's freedom.

Edward dropped his arm from his wife's shoulders and came to stand beside them as Jesse lifted the deposed attorney into the back of the sheriff's wagon. "Father," he said quietly.

"Oh, get out of my sight!" the man howled. "This is all your fault, you know. If only you'd stayed in the family business where you belonged. And married the woman you were supposed to marry. And let that foolish inn rot to the ground. But, no! You had to thwart my will again and again and again! You left me no choice, son. None at all, but to come out here and destroy the empire you tried to build. I almost succeeded, too. I would've bought up every inch of this mountain, just to enjoy watching it burn to the ground. I would've had every politician, lawman, and business owner in my back pocket. And I would've danced on top of the sepulcher of your failure."

"Not another word," Edward ordered, with a look of white-faced pleading in Jesse's direction. "I'll make sure you get a good lawyer."

"I *am* a lawyer, you nincompoop!" Penn Remington was all but foaming at the mouth.

As much as Jesse had dreamed about this day and looked forward to it, he suddenly realized that he didn't need the glory of marching Penn Remington all the way to his jail cell. He already had everything he wanted most. He had a wife who loved him and a son he adored more than his own life. He had his brothers and his own land. Thanks to the current round of arrests, he also suddenly and unexpectedly had his job and his personal freedom back. It was enough.

After loading Penn Remington into the wagon, he angled his head at the sheriff. "Do you mind taking it from here? There's something I need to handle before heading back to the station."

Despite the glow of triumph stamped across his features, Rick Dawson snorted. "I muddled through an entire year without you, deputy. I think I can survive another couple of hours."

As he and his other deputies rolled away with their prisoners, Jesse Hawling faced his long-time friend and foe. Edward Remington stared wordlessly back.

After a long silence, Jesse spoke first. "We've been through too much together to become enemies now."

There was no denying the hurt in Edward's gaze, though. "You didn't have to herd my father past all of these townsfolk like a mangy dog."

"No, but I sure wanted to," Jesse confessed. "I wanted him to pay for his many wrongs against my wife and me. For his wrongs against you, as well. And against all those innocent women. And all the evil things he had planned for our town. Then I saw your face and remembered he was your father and that you were my friend." Jesse shook his head soberly. "I'm sorry, Edward. I'm sorry for what that man did to both you and me. I'm sorry for—"

The hubbub of the rodeo grew sharply louder.

"Fight! Fight! Fight! Fight!" a chorus of men chanted.

Jesse glanced up in surprise as dozens of townsmen jogged across the snow in their direction.

Edward gave a mirthless laugh. "Should we indulge them?" He was already unbuttoning his jacket. Wrenching it off, he threw it down in the snow and started to roll up his white shirt-sleeves.

Jesse stared at him in amazement. "What are you doing?"

"Giving them what they want!" Edward growled. "It's what you want, too, isn't it? It's what everybody wants, a big brawl between the Remingtons and the Hawlings. Come on, Jesse, put up your dukes!" He crouched into a boxer's stance and started to dance around him in a semi-circle, throwing a few practice punches in the air.

Jesse read the blood in Edward's eyes and knew he wasn't going to get out of their confrontation unscathed. The innkeeper was too upset. He needed an outlet for all the rage simmering just beneath the surface.

"Good Lord Almighty, give me strength!" Jesse muttered beneath his breath as he faced his friend.

"That's it. Pray, you heathen!" Edward snarled. "Beg for mercy. You're going to need it."

"Whoa!" Pecos materialized and sprinted in their direction. "What do you two think you're doing?" He jumped between them, swinging his head back and forth to gauge Edward's angry expression and Jesse's rueful one. "This is a rodeo, not a boxing match, fellas!"

"Fight! Fight! Fight! Fight!" the roar of the men around them escalated to a throbbing war cry.

This is a rodeo, not a boxing match. Jesse blinked as inspiration struck. His head shot up to meet Pecos' furious gaze.

"You want a fight, eh? Alright, Edward Remington. You asked for it." He unbuckled his holster and threw it dramatically into the snow. Pointing at the horse ring, he snarled. "You and me. Alone in the ring with two bucking broncos. Whoever stays on the longest..." The rest of what he was about to say was drowned out by a roar of approval from their audience.

Casting a few furtive glances around them as they made their way to the ring, Jesse was amazed at how polarized their audience was. Over the past several months, he'd heard reports about it, but he hadn't really believed it until now.

Rabid fans of the Remingtons were clustered on one side of the ring, while equally loud and boisterous fans of the Hawling brothers were congregated on the other side. A body would've thought they were cheering on two boxers from the lather they worked themselves into.

The last thing Jesse saw before he entered the ring was a trio of women's faces — Lacey, Iris, and Meg were huddled together back at the bonfire, as if unable to bring themselves to witness what was about to happen up close. *Er, wait.* There was a fourth face with them, that of Mariana, the petite mother-to-be who'd single-handedly escaped from her captors and provided the information needed to bring them to justice.

None of the women were sobbing; they were simply pale with acceptance. Jesse's clash with Edward had been a long time coming. They knew it. Everyone knew it.

Pecos reclaimed the attention of his audience by running a pair of demonic Mustangs through the ring to demonstrate to his audience what was coming. Their roar of approval only grew louder. Men clapped, stomped, and shouted both encouragement to their favored rider and derision to his opponent.

Two small groups of Comanches separated Jesse and Edward and prepared them to enter the ring. The bucking broncos were returned to their chutes, and the two riders were placed atop them while the Natives held the beasts in check.

Pecos leaned over the railing to hand Jesse his rope. "It's not too late to change your mind." He spoke between clenched teeth. "We're all friends here. This is foolish, and you know it."

"It is," Jesse sighed, "but it's necessary. Edward just watched his father get arrested, and I'm the fellow who did it. He's in no mood to shake hands and be friendly. At least this is better than going at each other with fisticuffs."

"Is it?" Pecos demanded. He pointed at the empty horse ring. "This is no child's game, Jesse. What you and he are about to do is dangerous. Somebody could get hurt out there."

"I know, but this has gotta happen." Jesse tightly gripped the rope, gripping his knees around the beast beneath him. "Edward is my friend. If our roles were reversed, he would do this for me."

Shoot! Jesse was mad at himself all over again. Edward had been making sacrifices for the Hawling brothers the whole time he'd been living in Christmas Mountain. Jesse had just been too stubborn to see it. Visions of Edward's many acts of kindness raced through his head — starting with the way he'd hired him and his brothers to come work for him instead of running them off his inn property they were trying to jump a claim on.

"Three. Two. O-o-o-one!" The audience sang out the countdown. Then the gates of Jesse and Edward's respective chutes were thrown open.

Their two broncos pranced into the ring and began their dance of madness. Jesse's was a reddish-brown demon in horseflesh that bucked his hind legs in the air first. The moment they came crashing back to the ground, he launched off his forelegs, trying to unseat his rider. Jesse dug in his knees and fisted the single rope harness like a lifeline.

Edward's bronco was a white creature speckled with black. It soon became apparent that the black spots were simply mottling his fur. There were black spots in his wild heart as well, which he demonstrated by furiously rocking from his back hooves to his front hooves, again and again.

In seconds, Jesse became too dizzy to continue thinking. He could barely see. It was just him and the frenzied horse beneath him. Splashes of color. A cacophony of voices and sounds. A blur of movement.

Then, without warning, he was yanked free of the beast, and his body went sailing through the air. Somehow on some level, his brain managed to register the fact that Edward, too, had become unseated. The two men flew by each other in mid air.

"My friend!" Jesse didn't know if he shouted the words aloud, or if he only screamed them in his head. The next thing he knew, he was crashing into the ground. The breath was knocked clean from his chest. He lay there, stunned and motionless.

EPILOGUE

Christmas Day

Today is the day. Meg hadn't slept a wink the night before. Maybe it was because she was back in a guest room at the Christmas Mountain Inn, on a real mattress, where it was entirely too warm, cozy, comfortable, and safe. Alas, Lacey had insisted upon it, and Edward Remington's wife was one of those ladies you didn't argue with, because you didn't stand a chance of winning. She was too ladylike, kindhearted, generous, and ridiculously persuasive. Meg groaned as she glanced down at the frilly white night gown the woman had lent her. Was it wrong of her to wish she was simply back in her buckskins?

Or maybe she hadn't slept for two straight heartbeats last night because today was Christmas — the one day of the year Meg had dreaded the most while growing up. A girl without a home and a family had no reason to do anything but wish the holidays away...or at least pray they would pass by quickly.

Or maybe she was so jumpy and out of sorts because it was her wedding day. *Yes, that's probably it.* Glum thoughts crowded Meg's mind, taking a seat right next to her happiness at knowing she was about to become Pecos' wife. Today. Before high noon. In less than two hours. Yes, she was in love with the man; and yes, she was ready to become his bride. But, like Christmas, weddings were supposed to be celebrated by families, and Meg didn't have one of those. *Yet.*

Only when the warm trickle of tears slid down her cheeks, did she leap out of bed to put an end to her pity party. *Enough!* So there would be no father to walk her down the aisle. *Boohoo.* At least she would be walking straight into the arms of a man who loved her. It was enough. Or should have been... *Oh, my lands, woman! It's enough.*

Giving herself a very real shake, Meg stared at the pale green gown hanging on the hook beside her four-poster bed. It was time to wash her face and put it on. It was the nicest garment she owned, a gift from Lacey. It only made sense to wear it to her wedding.

As she moved to stand before it, however, a knock sounded on the door. Unaccountably relieved by the interruption, Meg hurried across the room to open it.

Lacey stood there, half-buried beneath the pile of fabric and frills in her arms. "Gracious! Take some of this off my hands," she gasped. "I'm begging you."

"Of course." Meg hastened to relieve her of most of the pile and spun around to toss it on the bed. She was alarmed to find Lacey leaning against the doorway, panting.

"Are you alright?" she cried, leaping forward to reach for her shoulders.

"I am." Lacey chuckled. "It's simply a bout of dizziness. It will pass."

"Why are you dizzy?" Meg demanded. Worry leaped into her chest.

"Not just dizzy. My stomach feels horrible, and lately I haven't been able to keep down a bite of food in the mornings. Plus, my clothes are too tight. Mercy!" Lacey waved a hand at her face, flushing prettily. "It's enjoyable being in the family way. And, by enjoyable, I mean it's not. Just hand me the precious little bundle, and be done with it, I say."

Meg had been blinking her way through Lacey's fascinating tirade, but she suddenly understood. "You're having a baby!" A tangle of emotions flooded her at the news — exorbitant happiness for the Remingtons mixed with a strange twist of envy.

"I am." Lacey waved both hands at her face and stepped away from the doorway, looking like a wood sprite in a high-waisted green velvet gown. "But there will be plenty enough time to plan for that. Today is about you and Pecos, and I have the perfect dress for you to wear."

Meg glanced over her shoulder at the dress hanging against the wall. "But I thought—"

"This!" Lacey stepped around her and lifted an ivory gown from the pile Meg had tossed atop the quilts. "We found it last summer inside an old chest in the attic. Isn't it lovely?"

Meg stared in awe as Lacey shook out the many layers of froth and lace. It was more than a gown. Putting it on was like stepping inside a gossamer cloud. It was something a princess might wear. Or the bride of a tribal chief, in her case.

"It's, ah...unbelievable," she stammered.

"It's perfect," Lacey declared in satisfaction. "Here. Let me tend to your hair. Mav will be here shortly to escort you down the stairs."

"Mav Peterson?" Meg gave a huff of disbelief.

"He's the only Mav we know," her friend retorted cheerfully. "At first, Jones was insisting he was the only fellow who could walk you down the aisle, but Pecos asked him to stand in as his best man, so...Mav offered."

She went to work on Meg's hair — brushing, combing, and primping. "The gown is old. You may wear my beaded combs in your hair for something new and borrow my crystal earrings for something blue. They're not overly blue, mind you, but there's definitely a hint of blue in there somewhere."

The next hour passed in a blur of happy chattering, mostly on Lacey's part, and the application of sweet smelling powders and creams.

Her friend finally stepped back, surveying her in satisfaction. "It's time."

Another knock sounded on the door. This time it was Mav Peterson, coming to escort her down the stairs. He was wearing his Sunday best black suit, which Meg happened to know he'd also worn to the last funeral in town. His wide, round features were tinged pink with pleasure, and his eyes were glowing.

"I never married, Meg. But, if I had, I'd count myself a thousand times blessed to have a daughter like you. You're a fine addition to our town, you are." He crooked a burly arm at her, admiring her dress. "Shall we, my dear?"

"Yes, please." Joy warmed her heart at the realization he was truly happy for her and truly happy to be a part of the special occasion. It suddenly no longer mattered that he wasn't her real father or that she didn't have a half dozen siblings milling around the parlor downstairs. She was living on Christmas Mountain around folks who truly cared for each other. Around folks who had each other's backs when it mattered the most. Around folks who might actually be closer knit in their hearts than blood relatives.

It was like walking in a dream as she clung to Mav's arm and sashayed down the inn stairs in her borrowed wedding dress. When they entered the parlor, she was amazed at how full of people it was.

My lands! She hadn't realized they possessed so many friends. There were Jesse and Iris with their baby, Jonah and Jack who had little Malachi perched on his shoulders, Sheriff

Dawson, Edward (who must have finally forgiven Jesse, since they were standing right next to each other), Lacey, Mav (of course), Sanko and Night Flyer, Dakota, and a dozen or so other Comanches looking mighty uncomfortable about being crammed inside the dainty parlor.

And at the front of the room beside the pianoforte was Pecos. Jones stood at his side, beaming as proudly as if the entire ceremony was his idea. She'd never before laid eyes on the man standing a stride behind them. His bronze features were lined with age and wisdom. She could only presume he was the presiding minister, since he wore a large silver cross around his neck. The rest of him was clad in familiar braids and buckskins.

Mav handed her off to Pecos, who eagerly placed her hand on his arm. Like her, he'd struck a compromise between the old and the new on their wedding day. He wore a freshly pressed white shirt like most of the other men in the room, but it was tucked into his buckskin leggings. He wore a brown leather vest over it and had his leather holster slung around his narrow hips.

While her hair was swept up, his was hanging straight and black down his back.

Meg hardly heard a word the minister said in his broken English. She was too busy holding the hands of the man she loved and drinking in the promises his coal eyes were making to her. She repeated her vows when she was prompted. He swore his life to hers next.

The minister spoke a blessing over them in a tongue she did not understand, and so they were married.

Pecos drew her close. Bending his head over hers, he declared huskily, "You are mine, Two Dark Moons, and I am yours." Then he touched his mouth to hers — as gently as the snow falling outside and as eagerly and adoringly as too many months of waiting can make a man.

THOUGH JONES WAS HAPPY FOR MEG AND PECOS, enormously happy, watching them exchange their vows left him with a lonely feeling. Now that Meg was wed, Pecos would come first with her, and where did that leave him?

Sure, it was a selfish thought, but Jones couldn't help it. He was alone. Again. It was the same sad story of his orphan boy life. The ceremony ended, and he was the first to congratulate the newlyweds. However, as other friends pressed closer, he backed toward the foyer, craving more breathing room.

He was so busy escaping the festivities that he almost didn't see the petite figure standing beside the Christmas tree. It was Mariana, but it was too late for him to avoid a collision.

"Pardon me, *bella*." Somehow he managed to dance a half step away from her in one direction while she danced a half step away in the other direction. They came to a halt, facing each other in the arched doorway. For the space of several heartbeats, all he could do was gawk, because the transformation in her was that astounding.

Someone had lent her a cherry red gown, gathered at the hem every few inches with beaded pins — probably because it otherwise would've been too long. They'd also let out the seams at the waist to give her blooming belly more room to, well, bloom.

"Merry Christmas, Deputy Storm." She peeped up at him shyly from beneath her glossy dark lashes.

Then, to his surprise and fascination, she placed her delicate hands on his chest and stood on her tiptoes to bring her face closer to his — closer but not nearly close enough. Her ball-like belly bumped into him, allowing her to go no further. She gave a breathy chuckle of defeat and waited.

"Mariana?" His heart thundered in his chest at her closeness. Though her flowery scent beckoned him closer, the fiercely determined look in her gaze puzzled him to no end.

She pointed above them. "Mistletoe. But you are tall."

"Ah." Finally perceiving the problem, he lightly clasped her upper arms and bent his head over hers. "Are you sure about this?" he whispered.

"*Mi héroe*," she murmured.

Her hero? Well, a fellow only had so much will-power. Jones covered her mouth with his, reveling in her sweetness. And, just like that, his heart slipped from his chest.

When he raised his head, he dazedly glanced down at her hands, half-expecting to see his heart clutched in them.

"Merry Christmas, Jones!" Meg sang out.

He was dimly aware of her and Pecos gliding past them. He had no idea where they were going. He was having trouble thinking in full sentences at the moment.

Jesse and Iris Hawling passed by him next. Though Jones couldn't yet muster the energy to pull his gaze away from Mariana's, he felt the deputy's firm clap on his back and heard his mocking, "Nice going, Romeo."

Ten Hours Later

"Can you believe the Remingtons and Hawlings aren't going to lift a finger to put a stop to all that nonsense about their supposed feud?"

Meg and Pecos were standing in the opening of the cavern that had served as his home for the past several years. Darkness was falling, and the stars were shimmering over the mountains.

Pecos gathered her into his embrace, dipping his head to

nuzzle the silky soft skin at her temple. "They're grown men. They'll do whatever they please." He started a trail of kisses at her hairline and traveled them down her cheek, around the side of her neck to her earlobe. He couldn't have cared less about whatever it was the Remingtons and Hawlings were up to this evening.

"It seems to me they've created a horrific uproar in town," she mused. "The villagers have all but drawn a line down the center of Christmas Mountain. The residents to the north of the line are the ones who were screaming Edward's name yesterday at the rodeo. And pretty much everyone south of the line were cheering Jesse on."

Pecos snorted, wondering what it was going to take to recapture his bride's attention and claim it for his own. "It's not a real feud," he reminded.

"To the townsfolk it is," she protested.

"Indeed it is. As it turns out, a good rip-roaring feud is good for business." He traced the curve of her cheek with his thumb. "Tickets are already sold out for our next two rodeos."

"Aren't you worried about the division it's creating? About the tangle we may be leaving for future generations?" she pressed, looking so worried that he paused his lovemaking to scowl down at her.

"They will sort through it, Two Dark Moons. Have a little faith. They will carve out a life for themselves and their families on this mountain just like we did. Sometimes they will clash. But good will always triumph over evil."

His thumb brushed across her lower lip. "And love will always find a way." With those words, he dipped his mouth to hers.

With a soft sigh, she finally gave in to the magic of the night. Winding her arms around his neck, she returned his kiss, proving his claim.

Their love had certainly found a way.

Thank you for reading
BRIDE FOR THE TRIBAL CHIEF.
Please leave a review!

Looking for more sweet historical romance books to binge read? Keep turning the page for a peek at more of my family and faith-filled romance series.

Much love,
Jovie

GET A FREE BOOK!

Join my mailing list to be the first to know about new releases, free books, special discount prices, Bonus Content, and giveaways.

https://BookHip.com/GNVABPD

NOTE FROM JOVIE

Guess what? I have some Bonus Content for you. Read a little more about the swoony cowboy heroes in my books by signing up for my mailing list.
There will be a special Bonus Content chapter for each new

book I write, just for my subscribers. Plus, you get a FREE book just for signing up!

Thank you for reading and loving my books.

JOIN CUPPA JO READERS!

If you're on Facebook, you're invited to join my group, Cuppa Jo Readers. Saddle up for some fun reader games and giveaways + book chats about my sweet and swoon-worthy cowboy book heroes!

https://www.facebook.com/groups/CuppaJoReaders

SNEAK PREVIEW: COWBOY
FOR ANNABELLE

To *protect her from a ruthless set of debt collectors, an impoverished southern belle agrees to become the mail-order bride of a rugged cowboy.*

After refusing to marry the cruel new owner of her childhood home, Annabelle Lane finds herself on the run from the scoundrels he hires to change her mind. In desperation, she signs a mail-order bride contract and hops on the next train, praying the groom she is matched with is a man worth running toward.

The most sought-after range rider in the west, Ethan Vasquez is highly skilled at protecting livestock from bears, wolves, and rustlers. But it's a job that leaves no time for courting, no matter how determined he is to have a family of his own someday. When a dare from friends has him scrambling to send off for a mail-order bride, he never imagines how quickly she will arrive or how much trouble will follow. It's a good thing he knows a thing or two about handling predators. He can only hope she finds his heavily scarred hands worth joining with hers in holy matrimony after the first wave of danger is past.

Cowboy for Annabelle
Grab your copy on Amazon. Read for FREE on Kindle Unlimited.

Read the whole trilogy!
MAIL ORDER BRIDES ON THE RUN
Cowboy for Annabelle
Cowboy for Penelope
Cowboy for Eliza Jane

Much love,
Jovie

SNEAK PEEK: ELIZABETH

Early November, 1866

Elizabeth Byrd rubbed icy hands up and down her arms beneath her threadbare navy wool cloak as she gingerly hopped down from the stagecoach. It was so much colder in northern Texas than it had been in Georgia. She gazed around her at the hard-packed earthen streets, scored by the ruts of many wagon wheels. They probably would have been soft and muddy if it weren't for the brisk winds swirling above them. Instead, they were stiff with cold and covered in a layer of frost that glinted like rosy crystals beneath the setting sun.

Plain, saltbox buildings of weathered gray planks hovered over the streets like watchful sentinels, as faded and tattered as the handful of citizens scurrying past — women in faded gingham dresses and bonnets along with a half-dozen or so men in work clothes and dusty top hats. More than likely, they were in a hurry to get home, since it was fast approaching the dinner hour. Her stomach rumbled out a contentious reminder at how long it had been since her own last meal.

So this was Cowboy Creek.

At least I'll fit in. She glanced ruefully down at her workaday brown dress and the scuffed toes of her boots. Perhaps, wearing the castoffs of her former maid, Lucy, wasn't the most brilliant idea she'd ever come up with. However, it was the only plan she'd been able to conjure up on such short notice. A young woman traveling alone couldn't be too careful these days. For her own safety, she'd wanted to attract as little attention as possible during her long journey west. It had worked. Few folks had given her more than a cursory glance the entire trip, leaving her plenty of time to silently berate herself for accepting the challenge of her dear friend, Caroline, to change her stars by becoming a mail-order bride like she and a few other friends had done the previous Christmas.

"Thanks to the war, there's nothing left for us here in Atlanta, love. You know it, and I know it," Caroline had chided gently. Then she'd leaned in to embrace her tenderly. "I know you miss him. We all do." She was referring to Elizabeth's fiancé who'd perished in battle. "But he would want you to go on and keep living. That means dusting off your broken heart and finding a man to marry while you're still young enough to have a family of your own."

She and her friends were in their early twenties, practically rusticating on the shelf in the eyes of those who'd once comprised the social elite in Atlanta. They were confirmed spinsters, yesterday's news, has-beens...

Well, only Elizabeth was now. Her friends had proven to be more adventurous than she was. They'd responded to the advert a year earlier, journeyed nearly all the way across the continent, and were now happily married.

Or so they claimed. Elizabeth was still skeptical about the notion of agreeing to marry a man she'd never met. However,

Caroline's latest letter had been full of nothing but praise about the successful matches she and their friends had made.

Be assured, dearest, that there are still scads of marriageable men lined up and waiting for you in Cowboy Creek. All you have to do is pack your bags and hop on a train. We cannot wait to see you again!

Caroline had been the one to discover this startling opportunity by reading an advert in The Western Gentlemen's Gazette. It had been placed there by a businessman who claimed to be running the fastest growing mail-order bride company in the west.

All I had to do is pack my bags and leave behind everyone and everything I've ever known to take part in the same opportunity. Elizabeth shivered and pulled her cloak more tightly around her. Attempting to duck her chin farther down inside the collar, she wondered if she'd just made the biggest mistake of her life. She was in Cowboy Creek several days later than she'd originally agreed to arrive, having wrestled like the dickens with her better judgment to make up her mind to join her friends.

Oh, how she missed the three of them! Caroline, Daphne, and Violet were former debutantes from Atlanta, like herself. All were from impoverished families whose properties and bank accounts had been devastated by the war. It was the only reason Elizabeth had been willing to even consider the foolish idea of joining them. She was fast running out of options. Her widowed mother was barely keeping food on the table for her three younger sisters.

Even so, it had been a last-minute decision, one she'd made too late to begin any correspondence with her intended groom. She didn't even know the man's name, only that he would be waiting for her in Cowboy Creek when her stagecoach rolled into town. Or so Caroline had promised.

With a sigh of resignation, Elizabeth reached down to grasp the handles of her two travel bags that the stage driver had unloaded for her. The rest of her belongings would arrive in the coming days. There'd been too many trunks to bring along by stage. In the meantime, she hoped and prayed she was doing the right thing for her loved ones. At worst, her reluctant decision to leave home meant one less mouth for Mama to feed. At best, she might claw her way back to some modicum of social significance and be in the position to help her family in some way. Some day...

Her hopes in that regard plummeted the second she laid eyes on the two men in the wagon rumbling in her direction. It was a rickety vehicle with no overhead covering. It creaked and groaned with each turn of its wheels, a problem that might have easily been solved with a squirt of oil. Then again, the heavily patched trousers of both men indicated they were as poor as church mice. More than likely, they didn't possess any extra coin for oil.

Of all the rotten luck! She bit her lower lip. *I'm about to marry a man as poor as myself.* So much for her hopes of improving her lot in life enough to send money home to Mama and the girls!

The driver slowed his team, a pair of red-brown geldings. They were much lovelier than the rattle-trap they were pulling. "Elizabeth Byrd, I presume?" he inquired in a rich baritone that was neither unpleasant nor overly warm and welcoming.

Her insides froze to a block of ice. This time, it wasn't because of the frigid temperatures of northern Texas. She recognized that face, that voice; and with them, came a flood of heart wrenching emotions.

"You!" she exclaimed. Her travel bags slid from her nerveless fingers to the ground once more. A hand flew to her heart, as she relived the sickening dread all over again that she'd experienced at the Battle of James Island. She was the unlucky nurse who'd delivered the message to Captain David Pemberton that his wife had passed during childbirth. The babe hadn't survived, either. But what, in heaven's name, was the tragic officer doing so far from home? Unless she was mistaken, his family was from the Ft. Sumpter area.

"Nurse Byrd." The captain handed his reins to the man sitting next to him, a grizzled older fellow who was dressed in a well-pressed brown suit, though both knees bore patches. "We meet again." He offered her a two-fingered salute and reached for her travel bags. He was even more handsome than she remembered, despite the well worn Stetson shading his piercing bourbon eyes. During their last encounter, he'd been clean shaven. His light brown sideburns now traveled down to a shortly clipped beard. If the offbeat rhythm of her heart was any indication, he wore the more rugged look rather nicely.

Which was neither here nor there. Elizabeth gave herself a mental shake. She'd been searching for a sign, anything that would shed light on whether she was doing the right thing by coming to Cowboy Creek. Encountering this man, of all people, only a handful of minutes after her arrival, seemed a pretty clear indication of just how horrible a mistake she'd made.

She nudged the handles of her bags with the toe of her boot to put them out of reach. "Y-you don't have to go through with this, captain. I can only imagine how difficult it is for you to lay eyes on me again." If it was anything close to how difficult it was for her to lay eyes on him, it would behoove them both to take off running in opposite directions. "I am quite happy to board with one of my friends until I can secure passage back to Georgia." The whole trip had been a horrible miscalculation of judgment. She could see that now as she stared stonily into the face of the officer who'd led the man to whom she was once affianced into the battle that had claimed his life. Captain Pemberton didn't know that wretched fact, of course. How could he? They were neither personally, nor closely, acquainted at the time.

The expression in his eyes softened a few degrees as he regarded her. "I gather you found the young man you were searching for during the war?" he noted quietly. "Otherwise, you would not be here."

Preparing to marry you, you mean! "I found him, yes." Her voice was tight with cold and misery. It was all she could do to keep her teeth from chattering. "I found him and buried him."

"Ah." He nodded sadly. "Words are never adequate in situations like these. Nevertheless, I am deeply sorry for your loss."

His regret appeared genuine. She sensed he was a kind man, a good man, despite the deplorable circumstances under which they'd made their first acquaintance. *More's the pity!* Though she couldn't exactly hold the captain responsible for the Union bullet that had taken her Charley's life, she couldn't just up and marry the man responsible for leading him into harm's way, either. Could she?

Perhaps it was the cold breeze numbing her brain, but suddenly she was no longer certain about a good number of things.

"Come, Elizabeth." The commanding note in David Pemberton's voice brooked no further arguments. "You must be famished after such a long journey, and you'll catch your death out here if we linger in the cold."

This time, Elizabeth's toes were too icy to function when he reached for her travel bags. She stood there shivering while he tossed them inside his wagon. She was both shocked and grateful when he proceeded to unbutton his overcoat and slide it around her shoulders.

It was toasty warm from his body heat and smelled

woodsy and masculine. "I th-thank y-you." She was no longer able to hide how badly her teeth were chattering.

"Think nothing of it, Miss Byrd." He slid a protective arm around her shoulders and guided her on down the street. "A friendly fellow named Frederick owns the eatery next door. Since our wedding isn't for another two hours, how about we head over there for a spell? We can grab a bite to eat and thaw out at the same time."

Our wedding? Her lips parted in protest, but she was shivering too hard to form any words.

As if sensing her confusion, he smiled and leaned closer to speak directly in her ear. His breath warmed her chilly lobe and sent a shot of...something straight down to her toes. "Surely an angel of mercy like yourself can spare the time to swap a few war stories with an old soldier?"

She clamped her teeth together. *An angel of mercy, indeed!* She'd felt more like an angel of death back there on the battlefield. There were days she lost more soldiers than the ones she managed to save. It was something she preferred never to think of again, much less discuss.

"If I cannot make you smile at least once in the next two hours, I'll purchase your passage back to Atlanta, myself," he teased, tightening his arm around her shoulders.

Now *that* was an offer she couldn't afford to pass up. She didn't currently possess the coin for a return trip, though she had to wonder if the shabbily dressed captain was any better for the funds, himself.

She gave him a tight-lipped nod and allowed him to lead her inside the eatery.

The tantalizing aromas of fresh-baked bread, hot cider, and some other delectable entrée assailed them, making her mouth water. A pine tree graced one corner of the dining area. Its boughs were weighed down with festive gingerbread ornaments and countless strands of red ribbon. A man in a white apron, whom she could only presume was Captain Pemberton's friend, Frederick, cut between a line of tables and hurried in their direction, arms outstretched. "You rebel you! Someone might have at least warned me you were one of the lucky fellers gittin' himself a new wife."

"Oh-h!" Elizabeth's voice came out as a warble of alarm as, from the corner of her eye, she watched a young serving woman heading their way from the opposite direction. She was bearing a tray with a tall cake and holding it in such a manner that she couldn't see over the top of it. She was very much at risk of running in to someone or something.

David Pemberton glanced down at her concern, but all she could do was wave her hand in the direction of the calamity about to take place.

His gaze swiftly followed where she pointed, just in time to watch the unfortunate server and her cake collide with Frederick. White icing and peach preserves flew everywhere. His hair and one side of his face were plastered with a layer of sticky whiteness.

The woman gave a strangled shriek and slid to her knees. A puppy dashed out of nowhere and began to lick the remains of the gooey fluff from her fingers.

Afterwards, Elizabeth would blame it on the long journey for frazzling her nerves to such an extent; because, otherwise, there was no excuse on heaven or earth for what she did next.

She laughed — hysterically! It was ill-mannered of her, unladylike to the extreme, and completely uncalled for, but she couldn't help it. She laughed until there were tears in her eyes.

Captain Pemberton grinned in unholy glee at her. There was such a delicious glint in his whiskey eyes that it made her knees tremble.

"A deal's a deal, nurse; and the way I see it, you did more than smile. You laughed, which means I'll not be needing to purchase that trip back to Atlanta for you, after all. Unless you've any further objections, we've a little less than two hours before we say our vows." He arched one dark brow at her in challenge.

Their gazes clashed, and the world beneath her shifted. As a woman of her word, she suddenly couldn't come up with any more reasons — not a blessed one — why they couldn't or shouldn't get married.

Tonight!

I hope you enjoyed this excerpt from
Elizabeth
Available now on in eBook, paperback, and Kindle Unlimited on Amazon.

Mail Order Brides of Cowboy Creek
Read the whole trilogy!
Elizabeth
Grace
Lilly

Much love,
Jovie

SNEAK PREVIEW: HOT-TEMPERED HANNAH

BOOK #1 IN THE MAIL ORDER BRIDES RESCUE SERIES

***A** bounty hunter is on the trail of a missing mail-order bride who looks identical to the only woman he's ever loved.*

When Gabe Donovan is recruited to track down a missing mail-order bride, he receives the shock of his life. She could pass as a twin to Hannah Merrill, the partner he thought he lost in a fire — the same woman he never got around to confessing his feelings to, for fear of ruining their partnership. If she's still alive, though, it means she must have faked her death to start over fresh some place else. Leaving him precious little time to track down the missing beauty before the past she's been running from finally catches up to her, and he loses her again...this time for good!

Heartwarming historical romance with a dash of humor, a twist of intrigue, and a happily-ever-after! Each title in this series can be read as a standalone.

I hope you enjoyed this quick peek at

Mail Order Brides Rescue Series:
Hot-Tempered Hannah.

Complete series — read them all!
#1: Hot-Tempered Hannah
#2: Cold-Feet Callie
#3: Fiery Felicity
#4: Misunderstood Meg
#5: Dare-Devil Daisy
#6: Outrageous Olivia
#7: Jinglebell Jane
#8: Absentminded Amelia
#9: Bookish Belinda
#10: Tenacious Trudy
#11: Meddlesome Madge
#12: Mismatched MaryAnne

Available now in eBook and paperback on Amazon + FREE in
Kindle Unlimited!

Much love,
Jovie

ALSO BY JOVIE

For the most up-to-date printable list of my sweet historical books:

Click here

or go to:

https://www.jografford.com/joviegracebooks

For the most up-to-date printable list of my sweet contemporary books:

Click here

or go to:

https://www.JoGrafford.com/books

ABOUT JOVIE

Jovie Grace is an Amazon bestselling author of sweet and inspirational historical romance books full of faith, family, and second chances. She also writes sweet contemporary romance as Jo Grafford.

Free Book!

Visit www.JoGrafford.com to sign up for my New Release Newsletter and receive a FREE copy of one of my sweet romance stories!

1.) Follow on Amazon!
amazon.com/author/jografford

2.) Join Cuppa Jo Readers!
https://www.facebook.com/groups/CuppaJoReaders

3.) Follow on Bookbub!
https://www.bookbub.com/authors/jo-grafford

4.) Follow on Instagram!

https://www.instagram.com/jografford/

5.) Follow on TikTok!

https://www.tiktok.com/@jograffordbooks

amazon.com/authors/jo-grafford

bookbub.com/authors/jo-grafford

facebook.com/JovieGraceBooks

instagram.com/jografford

pinterest.com/jografford

Made in the USA
Middletown, DE
04 November 2024